YAS

9/98

AIDS

Other titles in Diseases and People

ALLERGIES
ISBN 0-7660-1048-1

ANOREXIA AND BULIMIA
ISBN 0-7660-1047-3

ASTHMA
ISBN 0-89490-712-3

CHICKENPOX AND SHINGLES
ISBN 0-89490-715-8

COMMON COLD AND FLU
ISBN 0-89490-463-9

DEPRESSION
ISBN 0-89490-713-1

DIABETES
ISBN 0-89490-464-7

EPILEPSY
ISBN 0-7660-1049-X

HEART DISEASE
ISBN 0-7660-1051-1

HEPATITIS
ISBN 0-89490-467-1

LYME DISEASE
ISBN 0-7660-1052-X

MEASLES AND RUBELLA
ISBN 0-89490-714-X

MONONUCLEOSIS
ISBN 0-89490-466-3

RABIES
ISBN 0-89490-465-5

SICKLE CELL ANEMIA
ISBN 0-89490-711-5

TUBERCULOSIS
ISBN 0-89490-462-0

—Diseases and People—

AIDS

Janet Majure

Enslow Publishers, Inc.

44 Fadem Road   PO Box 38
Box 699   Aldershot
Springfield, NJ 07081   Hants GU12 6BP
USA   UK

Library of Congress Cataloging-in-Publication Data

Majure, Janet, 1954–
    AIDS / Janet Majure.
        p. cm. (Diseases and people)
    Includes bibliographical references and index.
    Summary: Discusses the history, diagnosis, causes, prevention, and treatment of a
disease that has affected more people over a wider geographic range than any other
epidemic.
    ISBN 0-7660-1182-8
    1. AIDS (Disease)—Juvenile literature. [1. AIDS (Disease)] I. Title. II. Series.
RC607.A26M337   1998
616.97'92—dc21   97-44139
                                                    CIP
                                                      AC

Printed in the United States of America

10 9 8 7 6 5 4 3 2 1

Illustration Credits: Centers for Disease Control and Prevention, pp. 15, 22, 24,
25, 26, 31, 37, 42, 44, 55, 64, 72, 80, 83, 101; © Corel Corporation, pp. 60, 74,
89, 94; National Institute of Allergy and Infectious Diseases, National Institutes of
Health, pp. 19, 52; Skjold Photographs, p. 46; World Health Organization, p. 10.

Cover Illustration: R. Feldman, National Institutes of Health

The cover image is a computer model of the HIV virus.

Contents

AIDS

What is it? *AIDS* stands for acquired immunodeficiency syndrome. AIDS is a set of symptoms that develops when a person's immune system becomes unable to fight off disease due to infection by the human immunodeficiency virus (HIV).

Who gets it? People of all ages and backgrounds get AIDS, although some people, such as people with multiple sex partners and injection drug users, are more likely to get it than others.

How do you get it? AIDS develops as a result of infection by HIV. A person gets HIV through contact with contaminated blood or other body fluids, and the virus is transmitted primarily through sexual intercourse and shared needles used by drug abusers. Pregnant women can pass HIV to their babies. Due to highly effective screening techniques, HIV is rarely passed through blood transfusions.

What are the symptoms? For an HIV infection to be classified as AIDS, a person must have a drastically reduced number of disease-fighting blood cells or develop certain opportunistic infections. These infections are caused by microbes that do not harm healthy people. Also, the purplish skin splotches of Kaposi's sarcoma, an extremely unusual cancer among the general population, is common among people with AIDS.

How is it treated? Treatments are constantly evolving but follow two basic paths. First is to provide preventive care to HIV-infected persons. Such care helps them avoid the opportunistic infections that are usually the direct cause of death in AIDS patients. The second is to try to disable the HIV with antiviral drugs. Disabling the virus keeps HIV from depleting patients' immune systems.

How can it be prevented? AIDS is almost totally preventable. A person can avoid AIDS by refusing risky behaviors. These behaviors include having unprotected sex, having multiple sex partners, and sharing needles used for injection drugs.

A Modern Epidemic

1

Earvin "Magic" Johnson is a basketball superstar and a multimillionaire. He is also a man with a history of having numerous sexual encounters with women. He announced in 1991 that he is infected with HIV, the AIDS-causing human immunodeficiency virus. The news shook the United States population, which had largely ignored the AIDS epidemic that began about 1982. People tended to regard AIDS as a "gay disease," since most early AIDS patients were homosexual white men. As a healthy, heterosexual athlete, Johnson changed people's perception of AIDS. The day after Johnson's announcement, callers overwhelmed AIDS hotlines. Callers wanted to know whether they might be infected and how they could get tested.

Unheard of twenty-five years ago, acquired immunodeficiency syndrome, or AIDS, today is ingrained in the consciousness of the world's population. No known epidemic has ever affected so many people over such a wide geographic range. Anyone can get it. Most people who get it die. Before they do, their body's ability to fight disease is killed. Patients typically suffer numerous debilitating illnesses, including pneumonia and cancer.

This epidemic so far has defied scientific efforts to find a cure or a vaccine. For now, prevention through safe human behavior is the only way to stop the spread of HIV.

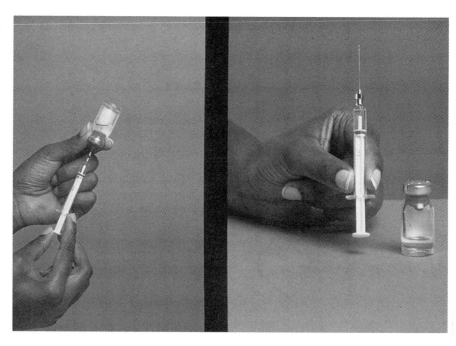

Although vaccines exist for many diseases, there is no vaccine or cure for AIDS.

An epidemic of such global proportions poses numerous difficult issues. In virtually every aspect of HIV and AIDS, good and valid goals compete with one another. Few questions raised by the disease have clear-cut answers, and matters of ethics often are at the heart of them. The questions include

- Which is more important: the broader public health or an individual's right to privacy? This question comes into play when deciding who should be tested for HIV and who should be informed of test results.
- Which is more important: helping the greatest number of people or making money? Ethically, one would argue that helping the most people is more important. In practical business terms, though, companies are not going to make health products for HIV and AIDS patients unless they will make a profit.
- Whose morality is more important? Should society provide condoms and clean needles to people who are likely to engage in premarital or homosexual sex or in the illegal use of injection drugs? Some people say that doing so would encourage immoral acts. Others say that failing to do whatever is necessary to prevent a fatal disease from spreading is immoral.

In the United States, citizens have made some decisions that have involved these ethical questions. For example, the federal government has ruled out mandatory HIV testing for nearly the entire population, although there are a few exceptions. Expense, low levels of usefulness, and individual rights won out over the possibility of identifying and, possibly, segregating infected individuals.

After a slow start, research dollars are now being poured into stopping AIDS. The task is difficult. HIV has proved to be a moving target. The virus changes, or mutates, very quickly, adapting to treatments applied to it. Scientists are making progress, however. Hope is emerging that AIDS can be controlled even if HIV is not stopped.

2

The History of AIDS

Long before AIDS became an epidemic, people were dying from it. One person was Robert R., a poor teenager in St. Louis, Missouri, who died in 1969. He appears to have been the first person in the United States to die from AIDS. During his illness, doctors were puzzled by his array of infections. The doctors saved blood and tissue samples in case new information later would shed light on his illness. In 1986, those samples showed that Robert had been infected with the human immunodeficiency virus (HIV). His many symptoms, including Kaposi's sarcoma lesions, indicated that Robert, who died at age fifteen, had AIDS. No one knows how or where he may have gotten it. No one thinks the condition began with him.[1]

HIV antibodies—an indication that a person has been infected with the AIDS-causing virus—have been identified in a 1959 sample of blood from an African person. Still, scientists cannot say for certain how or where the AIDS epidemic started. Many theories, such as the one about the mutation (or change) of a previously harmless virus, can explain the start, but none has been proved. Most evidence indicates the virus developed in Africa.[2]

The virus appears to have moved from Africa to Europe and then to the United States, thanks to fast and convenient modern-day transportation. The virus also made its way to Haiti when Haitians returned home after working for developing governments in Africa. Now AIDS is widespread in Africa, and cases have been reported on every continent except Antarctica.

Epidemic Explodes

Once HIV had reached the United States, the epidemic took off. An epidemic occurs when a disease spreads rapidly through a definable segment of the population. Disease-control officials in the United States labeled AIDS a new medical syndrome in June 1981 after several individuals died from a set of rare diseases. A syndrome is a set of symptoms that occur in combination. In the case of AIDS, the symptoms were rare diseases found only in people whose immune systems, which fight disease, are weak. Among the diseases were a type of pneumonia caused by a parasite and a cancer called Kaposi's sarcoma. (A later definition of AIDS symptoms included low counts of certain disease-fighting blood cells.)

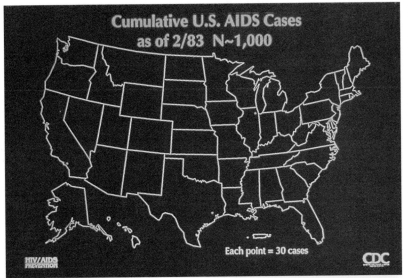

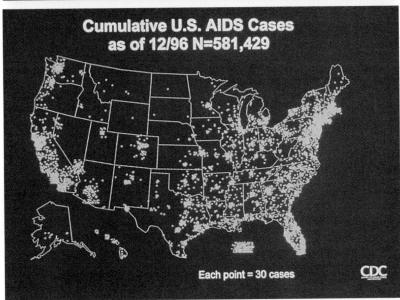

The number of AIDS cases in the United States has dramatically increased since 1983.

The epidemic moved rapidly. Before 1981, the year AIDS was identified, eighty-seven cases of the syndrome had been diagnosed in the United States. Of those patients, thirty had died. In just the first six months of 1981, thirty-seven more people died of AIDS.[3]

AIDS patients were identified by the unusual diseases that sickened them. Germs that are harmless to most people can cause grave illness among people whose immune systems do not work properly. Such were the diseases affecting AIDS patients. People with AIDS, however, did not fit into any known category of people with immune defects. The vast majority of AIDS patients were previously healthy young men. They were not people with compromised immune systems from taking drugs or radiation for cancer or arthritis. They were not children with inherited immune problems. Just the same, those young men were dying from extreme cases of rare diseases. Since the diseases the patients got were rare, few treatments existed for them.[4]

Health officials and private physicians, especially in New York, Los Angeles, and San Francisco, where the early cases occurred, were alarmed. They saw that the AIDS patients were men who had many unhealthy sexual contacts that could spread a disease. In particular, the patients had many sex partners, and they regularly engaged in anal intercourse. Those health officials knew that if a new contagion were causing the syndrome, hundreds of people besides those few patients probably would have been infected.[5] By the time the U.S. Centers for Disease Control and Prevention (CDC) declared an epidemic in September 1982, hundreds of people had already died and hundreds more were diagnosed with AIDS. The majority were homosexual men.[6]

Slow Response

Public health officials' response to the epidemic, however, was slow. Some scientists, physicians, and homosexual men thought AIDS was a sexually transmitted disease, and they argued strongly for public education to stop the spread of it. They wanted to tell people, particularly gay men, that they should avoid sexual contact altogether or that they should use condoms, a sort of rubber "glove" for the penis, when they had sexual contacts.

The early incidence of AIDS among gay men worked against public education efforts. Many public officials were uncomfortable with the idea of producing public education literature that included explicit sexual information. Some gay activists also opposed such materials, saying such efforts were actually intended to keep gay men from enjoying sex and to promote discrimination against them. Opponents of this kind of public education also argued that no one could prove AIDS was caused by a contagious microbe, a microscopic organism.

Soon people who were not gay developed AIDS, and scientists believed that the new patients had been infected through contaminated blood. If that were the case, it meant that many, many more people could have been exposed to AIDS than previously thought. Since many gay men were faithful blood donors, epidemiologists (people who study disease) feared some gay men were unknowingly passing AIDS through the blood supply. Such fears were realized when AIDS developed among people exposed to other people's blood. Those were individuals who had blood transfusions, people who injected illegal drugs and shared needles, infants born to women who injected drugs, and hemophiliacs. (Hemophiliacs are people whose blood does not clot properly. They regularly receive injections of a blood product, made from donated blood, that helps control bleeding.)[7]

Cause Identified

At last, in 1983, scientists identified a virus that causes the disease. The virus, which came to be called HIV (human immunodeficiency virus), was highly unusual. It was a retrovirus, a type of virus that reproduces by using a protein called reverse transcriptase. It was only the second retrovirus known to infect human beings, and only a handful of scientists had any experience with or knowledge of human retroviruses at that time.

In addition, HIV was unusual in that outwardly it did not harm victims for years. All the while, however, HIV would be destroying its primary victims inside the body. These victims were the CD4 lymphocytes (also known as helper T cells), a kind of white blood cell that is an important component in the body's immune system. Since HIV could exist unnoticed for years, epidemiologists knew that there were probably thousands of infected people who did not yet know they were

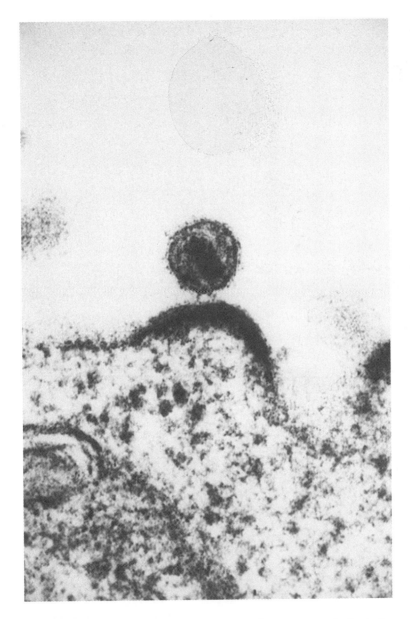

HIV, shown here as the circle leaving a CD4 cell, can exist in the body for years without harming the infected person.

infected. Those infected people could be passing on the disease through sex, shared needles, or blood donations.

Official Response

The early years of the United States epidemic are noted for the federal government's failure to respond as aggressively to it as it had with some other epidemics. AIDS began during the presidential administration of Ronald Reagan, whose policy was to cut spending on nonmilitary programs. Thus, funding requests by the CDC and some private physicians were largely ignored by government officials.[8] Disease-control specialists at the CDC were not given adequate funding to pursue their AIDS research leads. Bureaucratic delays and scientific competition also contributed to the slow governmental response.

Blood bank operators, meanwhile, did not want to restrict blood donations unless an infection was clearly identified. Because of these problems, the epidemic grew much larger than even the most pessimistic predictions.[9] By the end of 1984—just three years after the syndrome had been identified—almost eleven thousand people had been diagnosed with AIDS, and about half of those had died.[10]

Authors Peter S. Arno and Karyn L. Feiden, in their 1992 book *Against the Odds*, described the situation:

> It became the toughest health challenge of the twentieth century. A fatal illness was spiraling out of control. At first the political and scientific establishment was unable to respond. . . . The absence of forceful direction at the highest levels of government power has been nothing less

than criminal. . . . Conservatives in charge at the [Reagan] White House were so offended by gay lifestyles and sexual practices that a trickle was allowed to become a flood before any action was taken.[11]

Journalist Randy Shilts, in his book *And the Band Played On*, wrote,

> In those early years, the federal government viewed AIDS as a budget problem, local public health officials saw it as a political problem, gay leaders considered AIDS a public relations problem, and the news media regarded it as a homosexual problem that wouldn't interest anybody else. Consequently, few confronted AIDS for what it was, a profoundly threatening medical crisis.[12]

Since then, the epidemic has hit with full force. By June 1997, 604,176 individuals over age twelve had been diagnosed with AIDS in the United States. Of those, 62 percent, or 374,656, had died. In addition, 7,902 children age twelve and under had been diagnosed, of whom 4,602, or 58 percent, had died.[13] At last, public and private organizations started responding with increased spending for AIDS education and research. Great advances in treatment have been made since then, but much remains to be learned.

Trends in HIV Infection

HIV infection has been concentrated in identifiable groups, but those groups have evolved over time. Two thirds of people diagnosed with AIDS in 1985 were men whose only risk factor was having sex with other men. Intravenous (IV) drug users, and women who had sex with IV drug users,

AIDS Cases in Male Adolescents and Young Adults by Exposure Category, through 1997, United States

Exposure Category	13–19 years		20–24 years	
	N	%	N	%
Men who have sex with men	652	34	10,569	63
Injection drug use	118	6	2,101	12
Men who have sex with men and inject drugs	92	5	1,767	10
Hemophilia	725	37	602	4
Heterosexual contact	69	4	706	4
Transfusion recipient	83	4	104	1
Other/undetermined*	195	10	1,050	6
Total	1,934	100	16,899	100

*Includes patients pending medical record review; patients who died, were lost to follow-up, or declined interview; and patients with an undetermined exposure.

Courtesy of CDC

represented 19 percent of new AIDS cases that year. Hemophiliacs and people who had received blood transfusions or donated body tissues made up about 3 percent of the cases. About 60 percent of the infected people were non-Hispanic white people. About 25 percent were African American, and about 15 percent were Hispanic. By far, the largest group of AIDS patients were white homosexual men.

By the 1990s, the nature of the infected population had changed significantly in terms of ethnic characteristics. The 1995 HIV/AIDS Surveillance Report issued by the CDC noted "a shift in the epidemic from whites to minorities, especially blacks and Hispanics."[14] The report cited statistics showing that for the first time, the proportion of persons reported with AIDS who were black was equal to the proportion who were white (40 percent),[15] and in 1996 the proportion of AIDS patients who were black (41 percent) exceeded that of whites (38 percent). That year, blacks and Hispanics made up the most AIDS cases among both men (56 percent) and women (78 percent).[16]

Other numbers underscored how AIDS had become a disease of minority populations. In 1996, the number of AIDS patients for every 100,000 black people (89.7) was six times higher than the rate among whites (13.5 per 100,000) and two times higher than among Hispanics (41.3 per 100,000). Rates were lowest among American Indians/ Alaska Natives (10.7 per 100,000) and Asians/Pacific Islanders (5.9 per 100,000). And although they still were the largest group, men who had sex with men constituted just 50 percent of the new AIDS cases in 1996 among people ages thirteen and older.[17]

The shift to minority populations worries health officials. Prevention through education remains the best hope for stopping the epidemic. The change in characteristics of new AIDS patients suggests that prevention messages are failing to reach African and Hispanic Americans. This means that new efforts specifically appealing to African-American and Hispanic people must be emphasized. Also, more people are becoming infected through heterosexual intercourse, a statistic that is not being taken to heart by many sexually active people. Heterosexual contact as the source of HIV infection had grown to 13 percent of the new cases in 1996.[18]

AIDS Cases in Female Adolescents and Young Adults by Exposure Category, through 1997, United States

Exposure Category	13–19 years		20–24 years	
	N	%	N	%
Injection drug use	170	14	1,717	28
Hemophilia	10	1	14	<1
Heterosexual contact	631	53	3,264	54
Transfusion contact	83	7	113	2
Other/undetermined*	302	25	946	16
Total	1,196	100	6,054	100

*Includes patients pending medical record review; patients who died, were lost to follow-up, or declined interview; and patients with an undetermined exposure.

Courtesy of CDC

By 1996, women accounted for one in five new cases of AIDS, the largest share ever recorded. Nearly all the 7,500 children with AIDS acquired HIV infection from their mothers around the time of birth. Another group having high rates of HIV infection was prison inmates. Most of the infected inmates fell into one of the major risk groups (intravenous drug users, sex partners of intravenous drug users, or men who have sex with men).

As of July 1997, a very few people, only 52 of the 612,078 people diagnosed with AIDS in the United States, definitely became infected through their work. Nearly all of those were health care workers who accidentally got stuck with needles used on infected patients. An additional 114 health care workers became infected, possibly through on-the-job exposure, although the CDC could not determine that for certain.[19]

Recipients of blood, blood products such as clotting factor, blood components such as plasma, and tissue accounted for about one percent of the new cases among all youths and adults.

There was good news in 1997, though. AIDS deaths in the first half of 1997 were 44 percent lower than in the first half of 1996.[20]

New Concerns Arise

Despite advances in treating HIV infection and in slowing the epidemic's advance, health officials still have major concerns, especially about trends in infection rates. First, the fastest-growing category of HIV infection is through heterosexual sex

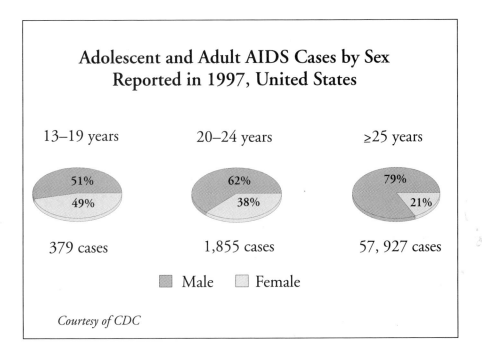

Adolescent and Adult AIDS Cases by Sex Reported in 1997, United States

13–19 years	20–24 years	≥25 years
51% / 49%	62% / 38%	79% / 21%
379 cases	1,855 cases	57, 927 cases

■ Male ☐ Female

Courtesy of CDC

contacts, especially in women. The heterosexual population far exceeds the gay population, so increases in heterosexual transmission rates are of particular concern. Worldwide, most HIV transmission is through heterosexual contact.

Also, the new concentration of AIDS among African-American and Hispanic people is an added concern, since they are more likely to have poorer access to medical care and information. On the average, people in those groups have lower incomes and education levels than the overall population. Another concern is that many IV drug-using women are prostitutes capable of passing the virus on to their many sexual contacts and to their babies, should the women become pregnant. Prostitutes' customers often have other

AIDS Cases in 13- to 19-Year Olds Reported in 1997 and 1996 Population Estimate of Adolescents by Race/Ethnicity, United States

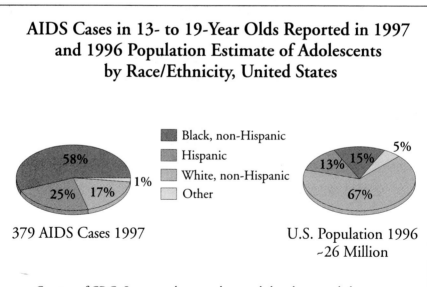

Courtesy of CDC. Some numbers may be rounded to the next whole percent.

sexual contacts as well, providing additional possibilities for the virus to spread.

The growth of HIV infection among teens and young adults is worrisome. Among all persons ages 25 to 44, HIV infection is the second leading cause of death, just behind accidents.[21] In 1995 alone, about three thousand new AIDS cases occurred in people ages 13 to 24, a significant increase. In 1997 the new AIDS cases for that age group fell to about twenty-two hundred.[22] Unfortunately, it is not clear whether the drop was due to young people behaving more responsibly or because better health care delayed the onset of AIDS among infected youths and young adults.

Meanwhile, AIDS has become a worldwide epidemic. Although the disease was first labeled an epidemic by the United States CDC, it now is concentrated in developing countries around the world. There, most HIV transmission is through heterosexual contact.[23] Also, most HIV varieties in developing countries appear more contagious than HIV sub-type B, the most common form of the virus in the United States.

3

What Is AIDS?

Much has been learned in the years since acquired immunodeficiency syndrome, or AIDS, was first identified in the United States. Perhaps the most important lesson is that it can strike anyone. "Anyone" includes people like Mary Fisher, a wealthy white woman and friend of former Republican presidents George Bush and Gerald Ford. Fisher was infected by her former husband, who died of AIDS and may have been an intravenous drug user. Fisher has become an outspoken speaker for AIDS awareness.

"I am not unusual," she said. "The point is, there are a lot of me's out there, women with small children who are [HIV] positive, women who are devastated, women who are scared to talk about it."[1]

Despite many obstacles, scientists have learned what causes AIDS, how the disease is spread, and how it can be prevented.

They have learned that AIDS, in fact, is the final and usually fatal stage of an infection that for years has few or no outward symptoms. Researchers now hope that the infection may be kept in check so that one day HIV infection can become a chronic—an ongoing but manageable—illness, as diabetes is for millions of people.

How the Virus Is Transmitted

HIV is carried primarily in blood, breast milk, semen, and vaginal secretions. It is transmitted through activities that cause those body fluids to enter the bloodstream of another person. That means a person is most likely to become infected through sexual contacts and shared intravenous needles and other IV drug paraphernalia. Infected women can also infect their babies during pregnancy or birth or while breast-feeding. A relatively small proportion of people have become infected through blood transfusions or by using blood products such as plasma. The virus can even be transmitted by unsterilized body piercing and tattoo instruments.

Being transfused with infected blood is the most efficient way of getting HIV infection, since transfusions require that a significant quantity of one person's blood be injected directly into another person's bloodstream. The possibility of getting HIV infection through donated blood or blood products, however, has been largely eliminated. Starting in 1985, blood centers have tested blood and plasma donations for HIV antibodies. The tests are more than 99 percent accurate, but some tainted blood occasionally goes undetected.[2] Hemophiliacs

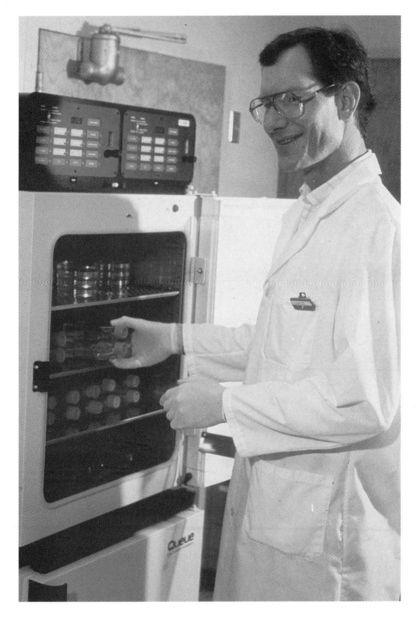

Through careful research, scientists have learned what causes AIDS and how it can be prevented.

are especially at risk, because they regularly use a product called blood clotting factor. Blood clotting factor is derived from many blood donations.

Unprotected sex with a man who engages in risky behaviors is by far the most common way HIV is transmitted. The riskiest sexual behavior is anal intercourse without a condom. Anal intercourse is when a man inserts his penis into a person's anus, or rectum, and ejaculates into the anus. This practice is common among gay men and probably accounts for most HIV infection among homosexuals. (Oral sex transmits HIV at a much lower rate.[3]) Since the walls of the rectum are relatively thin, tiny fissures or cuts can occur in the walls, allowing the infected semen to enter the bloodstream. A man can also infect a woman through vaginal intercourse, although transmission is somewhat less efficient since the walls of the vagina are thicker than those of the rectum. Fewer cases have been recorded of women passing HIV to men through heterosexual intercourse, but HIV is carried in menstrual blood and, although in small amounts, in vaginal secretions.

Sharing intravenous drug needles also has proved an efficient means of HIV transmission. A small amount of a person's blood is likely to be in or on the needle after an injection. When that needle is used again, that tiny bit of blood is often enough to infect the next user. The same risk applies to the paraphernalia (or "works") used for preparing drugs for injection.

About one fourth of HIV-infected women who become pregnant pass on the virus to their unborn babies. Researchers are uncertain exactly how the transmission occurs. They think the mother's blood that enters the umbilical cord is a likely vehicle. It is also possible for HIV-infected mothers to transmit the virus through breast milk. Drug treatments for mothers vastly reduce the transmission rate from infected women to their babies.

How HIV Works

When HIV enters the body, the virus first attaches itself to a CD4 lymphocyte, a kind of disease-fighting white blood cell.

HIV Is Easy to Avoid

People, understandably, are afraid of HIV infection, but the virus actually is very difficult to catch unless a person engages in high-risk behavior. The virus cannot survive for long periods outside the human body. It is not possible to become infected by sharing a toilet, by sneezing, or by living, working, or attending school with an infected person. A person cannot get AIDS from pets, from sex with an uninfected partner, or through closed-lip kissing. Some people worry about ways of transmission that are possible in theory, such as being bitten by a mosquito or touching an infected person's saliva. Scientists have found no instances of HIV being transmitted in these ways and believe them to be impossible for practical purposes. Health officials do recommend that people avoid sharing toothbrushes or razors with an infected person and avoid engaging in kissing that involves saliva exchange.

As a retrovirus, HIV is able to invade the CD4 cell's genes, which tell the cell how to reproduce. When HIV enters the genes, the cell begins to reproduce virus cells rather than disease-fighting CD4 cells. Eventually, the increased number of virus cells destroys the host cell and enters other CD4 cells in the body. In time, 80 to 90 percent of an infected person's CD4 cells die. Without the CD4 cells to fight disease, the patient is vulnerable to numerous infections, including those that cause opportunistic diseases. A combination of the resulting diseases, or a severe depletion of the CD4 cells, constitutes AIDS.

Researchers think HIV infects and weakens other parts of the body besides CD4 cells. These include monocytes, another kind of immune cell, which fight harmful bacteria. Also, HIV infects and weakens cells in the brain, skin, lungs, lymph nodes, and digestive tract, which is probably why those organs are especially prone to opportunistic infections and tumors when a person has HIV.[4]

Initial Infection

When a person is first infected with HIV, he or she will typically get sick two to six weeks later with what seems to be a bad cold. The person may feel tired and achy and have a fever, headache, sore throat, skin rash, and enlarged lymph glands, but the symptoms pass in a week or two. Lymph nodes or glands filter lymph, a clear body fluid that carries white blood cells throughout the body. Swollen lymph glands commonly indicate that the body is fighting an infection. They can be felt under the skin at the back and front of the neck and below the jaw line. Others can be felt in the armpits and groin.

As with most viral infections, the body responds to the invading virus by developing antibodies. (An antibody is a part of the immune system that attacks a specific bacterium or virus.) A person with HIV infection typically develops HIV antibodies six to twelve weeks after being infected. With most viruses, antibodies eliminate (or clear) the virus and guard against future infections by that same virus. As with a few viruses, though, the HIV virus survives even after antibodies develop. While a person infected with HIV carries on life as usual after the initial infection, the virus quietly multiplies inside the body and kills CD4 cells.

HIV and AIDS Symptoms

For the first five to ten years after becoming infected with HIV, the infected person typically shows no outward symptoms. However, he or she is contagious. The infected person can transmit the virus to other people through the exchange of body fluids during sexual contact or through blood. Unless the person's blood has been tested for HIV antibodies, however, no one would know the virus is being transmitted. Sometimes, infected people who are not yet seriously ill will experience swollen lymph nodes for months. There is evidence that a person is particularly contagious during the first two months or so of infection, before antibodies develop.

After five to ten years from the initial infection, although the time varies widely, infected people start showing signs of illness. They enter a middle phase of HIV infection in which they develop symptoms. Combined, these symptoms are called AIDS related complex, or ARC. ARC includes what doctors call chronic constitutional symptoms, such as ongoing weakness, tiredness, weight loss, diarrhea, and fever. About 80 percent may develop thrush, which causes painful white patches in the mouth and is seen only occasionally in anyone who is otherwise healthy. Night sweats, in which a sleeping person is suddenly drenched with sweat, often occur. Another common condition is herpes zoster, known as shingles, a painful skin condition caused by the same virus as chickenpox. Advances in medical treatments have prolonged this phase of HIV infection, and in the 1990s many people have been infected for more than ten years without developing AIDS.

The HIV infection is not considered to be AIDS until certain other conditions develop, usually two to three years after the appearance of thrush. The most common of these so-called AIDS indicator conditions is severe loss of CD4 cells, those disease-fighting white cells that HIV targets. About 85 percent of AIDS patients experience major CD4 losses. Other indicators include opportunistic infections. These infections occur among people whose weakened immune systems are unable to fight off common bacteria, viruses, and other microscopic organisms.

The most common of these infections is *Pneumocystis carinii* pneumonia, or PCP, a lung infection caused by a parasite.

Other serious opportunistic infections include toxoplasmic encephalitis, a brain infection caused by another parasite. Also, cytomegalovirus (CMV) infection is carried in blood cells and can cause symptoms in many different organs, from encephalitis in the brain to diarrhea in the digestive tract. CMV can also cause infections in the eye and the liver. The most common opportunistic tumor (abnormal growth) that appears in AIDS patients is a cancer known as Kaposi's sarcoma. Frequently, Kaposi's sarcoma is evident by purplish skin lesions.

Several other ailments also can indicate AIDS. These include cancer of the cervix (which connects a woman's vagina

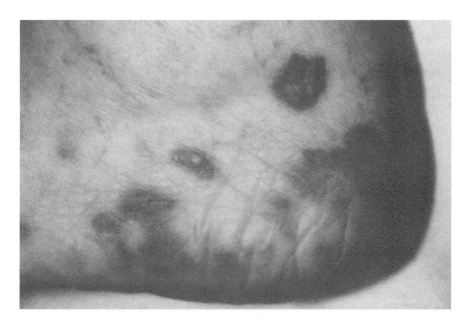

Kaposi's sarcoma, shown here on the heel of a foot, is a skin cancer that is often seen in AIDS patients.

and uterus), recurrent pneumonia, and dementia, in which a person may hallucinate, become severely depressed, or suffer memory loss. Tuberculosis, or TB, also has developed in people with AIDS, which creates an added concern. Unlike other AIDS conditions, TB can be spread to people who do not have suppressed immune systems, although people with weakened immunity are more susceptible to it.

Infected people do seem to have a lower chance of death if they take medications that attack retroviruses and that prevent *Pneumocystis carinii* pneumonia. Also, HIV infection advances more quickly in individuals who have a large amount of the virus in their blood than in those with less virus.[5]

4

Diagnosing HIV Infection

Gossip columnists and Hollywood watchers had been speculating for months about the cause of movie star Rock Hudson's ill health. In his last public appearance, in July 1985, the square-jawed romantic hero was thin, drawn, and weak. Seven days later, Hudson collapsed in Paris, where he had secretly gone to seek treatment for AIDS. His AIDS diagnosis was announced publicly a few days later, prompting the first front-page news coverage of the epidemic.

Just a few years earlier, the diagnosis would not have been possible. Acquired immunodeficiency syndrome was first identified as a medical condition in 1981. As a syndrome, AIDS is not a disease but, rather, a collection of symptoms that occur together.

AIDS is diagnosed when a person exhibits the particular set of signs or symptoms that define acquired immunodeficiency syndrome. As mentioned in Chapter 3, those AIDS-defining signs and symptoms include a severe reduction in CD4 cells and several opportunistic diseases. By the time AIDS is diagnosed, doctors and patients can do little to stop its progress.

Diagnosing an HIV infection, however, is readily achieved. Doing so before the infection develops into AIDS is critical to better health. A person who knows he or she is infected with HIV can take treatments to reduce the chances of developing a life-threatening opportunistic infection. In addition, an infected person can take steps to make sure that he or she does not spread the infection.

Developing a Test for HIV

Developing a blood test for HIV became the top United States research priority as soon as the virus was identified in 1983. A test for HIV antibodies, which became available to researchers in 1984, addressed two immediate needs: renewing the safety of the blood supply and giving epidemiologists a better idea of the size and range of the epidemic.[1]

The first HIV-antibody test licensed for use and the most widely used test today is known as ELISA (enzyme linked immunosorbent assay). ELISA is safe, reliable, and simple. Typically, clinicians send a sample of a patient's blood to a laboratory for analysis. Normally, when a sample tests positive (meaning HIV antibodies are present), laboratories repeat the test to double-check. After a second positive result, the sample is then subjected to another test, called the Western blot.

This three-test procedure is nearly 100 percent accurate for positive identification of HIV antibodies. If results are at all unclear, the laboratory may label the test as inconclusive.[2] Patients may be advised to provide another blood sample for testing after a few months.

The test is not entirely accurate, though, because it tests for antibodies rather than for the virus itself. A person recently exposed to the virus may be infected even though he or she has not yet developed antibodies. Antibodies may not appear for six to twelve weeks. People at risk because of their sexual or drug-use activities are encouraged to stop their risky behaviors and be tested again after six months or so, after HIV antibodies have been given a chance to develop.

Results from this kind of testing usually are not available for about two weeks. Many people seek anonymous testing. They then must return to the testing site to get their results. Almost half never go back. Public health officials worry about the low return rate. They are concerned that the people who do not return will continue to engage in the unsafe sex or drug activities that prompted them to get tested. Officials also worry that the people who are unknowingly HIV-positive (another term for being infected with HIV) will miss out on early treatment possibilities. People who give blood—who must give their names and addresses—are notified to return for a retest if their blood test results are HIV-positive. Donated blood is not used until testing has been completed.

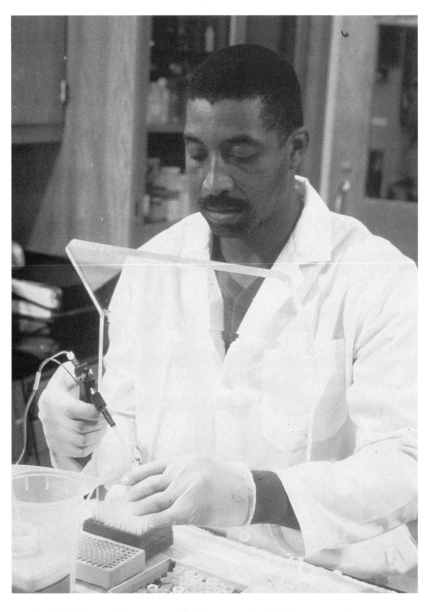

A technician performs a standard enzyme linked immunosorbent assay (ELISA), the most widely used test for HIV antibody.

Other HIV Tests

A different kind of HIV test is very effective but very expensive. That test, the polymerase chain reaction (PCR), can count the actual amount of HIV (the viral load) in a person's blood, as opposed to detecting antibodies. Thus, it can identify infection even before antibodies have formed. The test, besides being expensive, requires strict steps to be taken to avoid contamination with positive samples, since it is so highly sensitive. PCR is used mostly by researchers to diagnose HIV, but it is also widely used by doctors to follow the level of virus in a patient using antiviral drugs.

Activists are calling for ways to make PCR more widely available, since viral load appears to be the best measure of how far a person's HIV infection has advanced. Also, a doctor and patient have a better idea of when to use or change antiviral drug therapies when they know the viral load. The Food and Drug Administration has approved the Amplicor viral load test and is likely to approve two other tests that provide counts of viral RNA in people's blood. (RNA is involved in transmitting genetic information when the virus reproduces.) Approval of the tests would also mean that insurance companies most likely would cover their costs.

A testing kit for home use, called Confide®, was approved for sale in May 1996 after long controversy. The kit, initially available only in Texas and Florida, allows the user to take his or her own blood sample. The user then mails the sample to a laboratory, which tests it, using ELISA. A few days later, the home-test user can call a toll-free telephone number and learn

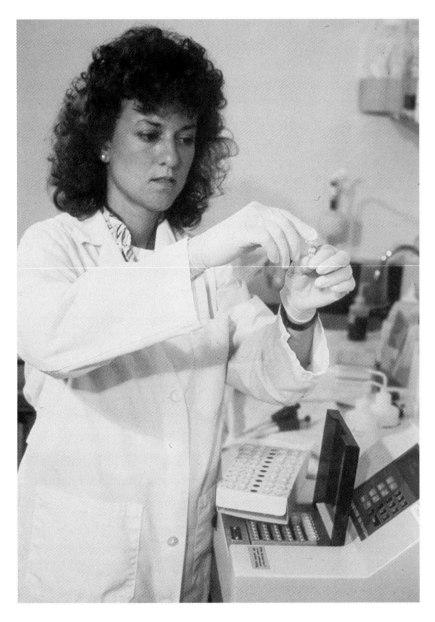

This technician is performing the polymerase chain reaction (PCR) test to count the actual amount of HIV in a blood sample.

the test results anonymously. Counselors provide support and guidance for customers. Home tests have been technically available for several years. During that time, the Food and Drug Administration had refused to approve such kits for fear that the test would be used improperly.

Other kinds of tests are also available. For example, one test looks for the antibody-dissociated p24 antigen, a protein found only with HIV that stimulates the body's immune system. Presence of the antigen is used for early diagnosis in newborns. Some newborns may not have HIV infection but test positive because they possess HIV antibodies passed on to them by their mothers. This test helps medical personnel to distinguish those babies from ones who are actually infected. Saliva-based tests have been approved for screening, although they are less sensitive than ELISA. As a result, a blood test is required to make a definite HIV-infection diagnosis.[3]

A rapid HIV test also is on the horizon. A study announced in September 1996 found that a ten-minute test was as accurate as ELISA. Health officials are hopeful that manufacturers will make the test available to clinics so that patients can receive almost immediate counseling. The test could solve the problem of people not returning to learn their test results.[4] The rapid test has not been approved yet by the Food and Drug Administration, although it is used in other countries.

Testing Recommendations

As of 1996, federal guidelines recommend counseling and testing for all pregnant women but emphasize testing should

A home-test kit for HIV allows a patient to call and anonymously learn the test results.

be voluntary. Some people worry, however, that testing for pregnant women will be made mandatory.[5] The argument for testing pregnant women is that if they are infected, they could then take AZT (an antiviral compound that is also called ZDV, or zidovudine). AZT greatly reduces HIV transmission during pregnancy or delivery. Without AZT, about 25 percent of infected women will have infected babies. With AZT, only about 8 percent of the babies are infected.

Meanwhile, a 1996 study found that the amount of HIV in the body, the viral load, is a good indicator of whether an infected mother will transmit HIV to her infant. If the study's conclusions are correct, that information could encourage more women to be tested. As it is, a woman might decide not to get tested because she does not want to undergo the AZT treatment and unpleasant side effects. However, doctors think that if a woman has a better idea of whether her baby will be infected, she might be persuaded to get tested.

Other candidates for routine testing are hospital patients between the ages of 15 and 54. The CDC recommends routine counseling and testing of that age group at hospitals where HIV infection is at least one percent or where at least one in 1,000 patients has AIDS. The idea is to find people who are unaware of their infection, to provide early treatment, and to teach people how to avoid infecting others. Officials estimate about 3 million people a year would be tested, and about 110,000 new HIV infections would be detected in the United States if hospitals follow the recommendation.[6]

Treatment

In the years since AIDS was first identified, treatment problems have been almost as numerous as the diseases that AIDS patients develop. Despite the many difficulties that researchers and physicians have struggled with, AIDS patients in the late 1990s have lived longer and better than the AIDS patients of the 1980s. Researchers continue to pursue efforts to better understand HIV—how it infects people and how to cope with the infection. Meanwhile, other scientists work to prevent and treat the opportunistic infections that HIV patients get.

The job is a difficult one, as the federal Agency for Health Care Policy and Research noted.

> Originally identified in homosexual men, [HIV] now increasingly affects men and women of all races, ethnicities, and sexual orientations, as well as infants, children, and adolescents. The obstacles to ensuring adequate care for

these diverse populations, and the complexity of care for each individual, make HIV infection one of the greatest challenges of our time.[1]

Still, scientists are cautiously optimistic that truly significant advances lie ahead.

Life with HIV Infection

Life becomes complicated when a person learns he or she is HIV-positive. As if the emotional toll of the news were not enough, a person's entire lifestyle often must change to stay healthy. Staying healthy is not easy. It often involves taking many medications and avoiding many activities that might cause illness.

Hydeia Broadbent, thirteen, told children at a Washington-area elementary school that the drugs she takes often make her sick. "When I get sick, I throw up, I get a headache, I'm cold," she said. "You know when you get a shot? It's 10 times that, it's 10 million times that. That's how I feel."[2]

When a person initially learns of being infected with HIV, his or her care largely consists of counseling and a thorough physical examination. The counseling includes advice on how to avoid spreading the virus and how to avoid getting sick. Although many people worry about catching HIV from an infected person, the infected person actually has many more worries. The microorganisms that cause opportunistic infections are almost everywhere.

Proper cautions against possible infections create limits on the lifestyles of HIV-infected persons. Depending on the degree to which the virus has affected their immune systems, infected persons might consider avoiding certain jobs where they could be exposed to diseases that prey on HIV-infected persons. These jobs include health care (to avoid tuberculosis and other infectious diseases), child care (to avoid cytomegalovirus, a common opportunistic infection, and other infections passed through human wastes), or work with young farm animals (to avoid cryptosporidiosis, another AIDS-related disease). HIV-positive people can get infections found in soil, which harbors assorted bacteria and other microorganisms. Pets present possible hazards because of microorganisms they may carry. HIV-positive individuals must use good hygiene in the kitchen. They must make sure to thoroughly cook eggs and meats to kill bacteria that might make them sick. Even some tap water, as well as water in lakes or streams, sometimes carries microorganisms that will make an infected person sick. People with HIV should not swallow water from rivers, lakes, or untreated swimming pools. Traveling poses extra risks, since it exposes a person to many different people and microorganisms that can cause illness.

Everyone infected with HIV is encouraged to get a pneumococcal vaccine to guard against pneumonia. Annual flu shots are also recommended. Vaccines for hepatitis B are urged for those who may be at risk for hepatitis B because of sexual contacts, needle-sharing, or poor personal hygiene.[3]

Overall good hygiene becomes very important to infected persons. They need to wash their hands well after contact with pets and raw foods. Exercise benefits HIV patients' health and

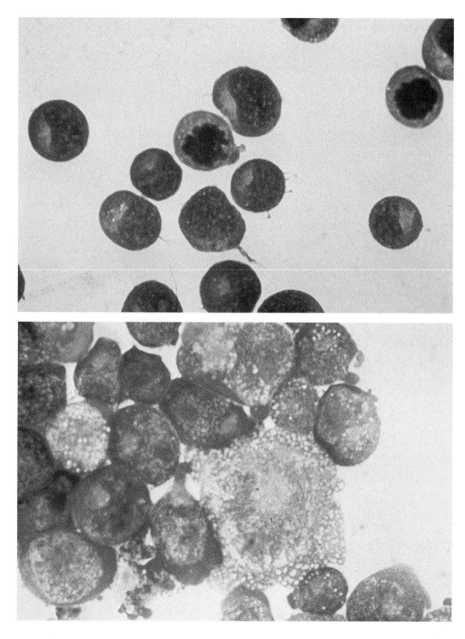

Normal CD4 cells are shown at the top, and CD4 cells infected with the HIV virus are shown at the bottom.

mood.[4] A healthy diet and avoiding alcohol also are helpful in building a strong immune system.[5]

Today's Treatments

AIDS clinics have developed a fairly standard treatment program for people with HIV. Doctors caring for people with HIV infection monitor the patients' blood levels of CD4 cells. When CD4 levels drop, it indicates that the immune system is weakening. A normal CD4 cell count is in the range of 600 to 1200 cells per cubic millimeter, and a count below 200 indicates an AIDS level of immune suppression. Viral load is a more reliable indicator of how far HIV has progressed in a person's body, but the test for viral load is generally less available than the CD4 count. Experts also encourage doctors to note patients' moods, since depression and suicide are more common among infected individuals than in the general population.[6]

Once a person's CD4 cell count falls below 200, doctors begin prescribing preventive treatments for some common opportunistic infections. Since opportunistic infections, rather than HIV, usually kill AIDS patients, treatments for those infections have played a key role in prolonging the lives of infected people. These patients take a common antibiotic combination, TMP/SMX (commonly known as Bactrim), to avoid infection by the *Pneumocystis carinii* parasite. Preventive drugs also are available to people who get a positive reaction to a tuberculin skin test. When the CD4 cell count falls farther, drug treatments are available against several other opportunistic infections.[7] Drug treatments are also available against repeats of the opportunistic infections.[8] Recently, a virus associated with Kaposi's sarcoma has been identified, which may lead to new therapies.[9]

Treatment for newborns and children varies somewhat from treatments for adults and adolescents. One reason is that AIDS symptoms usually begin within a year for infected infants, and they die sooner than adolescents or adults with HIV. AIDS is the sixth leading cause of death among children ages one to four. However, of eleven drugs available to treat AIDS, only six have been approved for children. Also, federal guidelines on using some of the newest AIDS treatments include special notes of caution for use in children. Caution is necessary because testing among children has been limited, and doctors, therefore, do not know for sure how the medications will affect children. AIDS activists are calling for more pediatric drug testing.[10] The Clinton administration has proposed a new rule requiring companies to test drugs on adults and children at the same time. In addition, newborns and children are susceptible to some different illnesses from those of adults and adolescents. As a result, preventive medical care can vary for them, too. Research continues for added pediatric therapies.[11]

Antiviral Treatments for HIV

In 1984, the National Cancer Institute set up a systematic screening process of existing chemical compounds, which led to the identification of the first known treatment for HIV. In

The automated ELISA test can indicate that a patient has HIV. After diagnosis, it is important that the patient avoid infection by opportunistic infections, such as pneumonia and cytomegalovirus.

1985, screening found that AZT extended the lives of people who already had developed AIDS.[12] A few years of widespread use of AZT and added research reduced the initial excitement that accompanied the drug's release in 1987. About half of the patients could not take it for long periods of time because they developed severe anemia (a deficiency of oxygen-carrying red blood cells) or other side effects. Also, many patients' infections became resistant to the drug after two to three years.[13]

Besides screening existing drugs, researchers also try to invent new drugs to stop HIV from reproducing. An especially exciting development in 1996 was the discovery that a combination of drugs can be highly effective. This combination was nicknamed the anti-HIV cocktail. One study found that infected people taking a particular combination of two nucleoside analogs and a protease inhibitor experienced a two-hundred-fold reduction in viral RNA. (Some tests identify viral load by the virus's RNA, part of the virus's genetic code.) In fact, in 86 percent of those patients, the virus became undetectable after treatment. Scientists think some of the virus was probably still in the patients' blood, but the test that measures HIV counts cannot accurately detect the virus if there are fewer than five hundred RNA copies per milliliter of blood. The people in the study had started out with more than two hundred thousand copies per milliliter.[14]

Many scientists warned people not to regard the viral reduction as a cure. By 1997, more sensitive tests detected that the virus was still present in patients. In addition, the expected rebuilding of patients' immune systems has been less successful than had been hoped. Adding to these disappointments have been difficulties in maintaining the three-drug regimen. It involves taking dozens of pills daily. Many of the drugs have serious side effects, interact badly with other drugs, and involve diet restrictions. Some 40 percent of the cocktail's failures have been blamed on patients' failure to take their medication correctly. On top of that, HIV readily mutates, or changes, and it appears able to develop resistance even to some of the latest drugs. Doctors are worried that they will not have a steady supply of new drug weapons against resistant HIV.[15]

Other Treatment Factors

The experience of doctors and hospitals in treating AIDS has a significant effect on patients' well-being. A study in January 1996 found that a patient's survival time is directly linked to his or her doctor's experience in treating patients with AIDS.[16] Also, AIDS patients have a lower death rate at hospitals that admit more AIDS patients than others.[17] The experienced doctors were more likely to monitor CD4 cell counts, prescribe drugs to prevent pneumonia, and provide more aggressive antiretroviral therapy. The message from the study is that most primary care physicians need more information. Most of them have had no formal training in AIDS treatment.[18]

Drugs Target Viral Reproduction

Various drugs try to stop HIV at different stages in its reproductive cycle. An enzyme (a special kind of protein) in HIV called reverse transcriptase contributes to the reproduction. Thus, some research has targeted reverse transcriptase; AZT and other drugs called "nucleoside analogs" work at this point in viral reproduction. An enzyme called integrase is another drug research target. A newly approved group of drugs called protease inhibitors attempts to block viral reproduction at another stage. The FDA now has approved several "antiretroviral" drugs that attempt to stop HIV from reproducing in the patient's body.

Patients also are likely to maintain better health longer if they have access to good health care. Early surveys hinted that HIV infection progressed faster in women and minorities. *Science News* reported in 1995 that sex and race were not the key to the difference in health. "Rather, unequal access to medical care may explain why some HIV-infected people stay healthier and survive longer than others," the article said.[19] That finding means that health care providers and public policy makers must actively work to assure that everyone has equal access to care if they hope to extend the lives of all AIDS patients.

Costs of Treatment

Costs, however, make equal access unlikely, since HIV and AIDS treatments are very expensive. Since AZT was first approved for marketing, costs associated with HIV treatments have been a source of controversy. Burroughs-Wellcome, the company licensed to sell AZT, initially sold the drug for $10,000 a year. Wide protests and major public demonstrations, notably by the patient advocacy group AIDS Coalition to Unleash Power (ACT-UP), led Burroughs-Wellcome to reduce its price.[20]

Since drug combinations now appear to be the most promising therapy, costs are an even greater concern. The anti-HIV cocktail costs $12,000 to $18,000 a year. Add to that the many other medications that patients with advanced AIDS may need, and the annual bill could rise to $70,000.[21] Health insurance companies will pay some of those costs, as will

Medicaid (the federal health program for people with substandard income). The federal Ryan White Act, a law named for a young man who died from AIDS, also provides money to pay for some AIDS treatments. These funding sources still leave many gaps in payment. Many people have to pay their own way, and, clearly, few people have that much extra money. Another added cost is the viral load test, which is expected to cost about $200 apiece once it is widely available for sale. That test would need to be used about four times a year for each patient.[22]

Financial considerations are playing a role in treatment decisions. Peter Hawley, medical director for the Whitman-Walker AIDS Clinic in Washington, D.C., told *American Medical News*, "[Treatment is] expensive . . . and it's complicated . . . and there is no sense starting someone [who] is not going to be able to continue." He noted that a growing gap exists between those who can and cannot get treatment.[23]

Alternative Treatments

About one third of HIV-positive individuals also turn to alternative therapies. Alternative therapies are those that have not been proved effective through controlled scientific tests. Infected people turn to them for many reasons, including failure of approved treatments and a desire to feel in control of their lives.[24]

Some alternative therapies improve the quality of life for many HIV patients. For example, yoga, acupuncture, massage, and meditation help patients deal with the stress related to their conditions and may improve their sense of well-being.[25] Other alternative therapies, such as herbal preparations, vitamins, garlic, and blue-green algae, may or may not help. Some may be harmful.

Alternative therapies also include underground drugs— drugs that are not yet approved by the FDA or are still being tested.[26] Another form of alternative treatment is unconventional uses of existing drugs. These include Antabuse, which is used for treating alcoholism, and Tagamet, a drug used for stomach ulcers. Tests have found that Tagamet provides no benefit. Antabuse is supposed to provide antiviral activity by linking with certain HIV proteins. No one knows, though, whether it works.

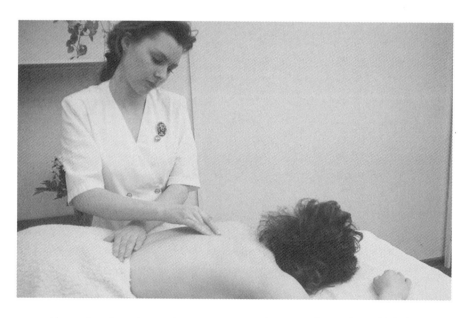

Alternative therapies, such as massage, can improve the quality of life for some AIDS patients.

Alternative treatments can have one benefit that traditional medicine may not for some AIDS patients. Studies find that people who believe in their treatments and actively participate in them get better results than those who do not.[27] Many AIDS patients are suspicious of the government and the science institutions and pharmaceutical companies that develop and test drugs. Those patients, thus, do not get the greatest possible benefit from their approved treatments. If those patients believe in and help choose their therapies, whether approved or alternative, they will get better results.

6

Prevention

While scientists work to develop a vaccine and a cure for HIV infection, prevention remains the only certain way to avoid AIDS. Prevention is both very simple and very difficult. The way to prevent AIDS is, simply, for people to stop having unprotected sex, stop sharing drug-injecting equipment, and stop having babies if they are infected. The complicated part, of course, is getting people to take those actions.

For a long time, most people thought AIDS was something that happened to people unlike themselves. Indeed, AIDS continues to be perceived as a disease of gay men and drug addicts. That attitude has caused many people, particularly women and young heterosexuals of both sexes, to believe that AIDS precautions do not apply to them. Thousands have learned that they were wrong, perhaps fatally so. While the

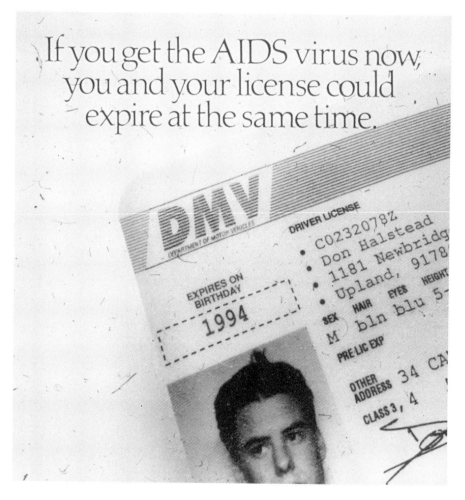

As this AIDS prevention poster from the U.S. Centers for Disease Control and Prevention suggests, AIDS is deadly.

rate of HIV infection has slowed, infection still continues to increase. Calls for stronger prevention efforts are nearly universal.

A group of teens in Jamestown, New York, learned the terrible lesson of unprotected sex in 1997. Nine young women in that small town were infected with HIV by one man. The youngest was fourteen years old. A young man contracted the virus after having sex with one of the girls. All nine girls had had sex with Nushawn Williams, a twenty-year-old drifter who gave compliments and, sometimes, drugs to the girls. Officials estimated that more than one hundred people were at risk through direct contact with Williams or through sex with one of his partners.[1]

Another man, Jim Johnson, trusted a partner who was actually cheating on him. The partner got HIV, and then Johnson did, too. Johnson said, "I thought I was totally invincible. I was 24 years old." Although he was angry at his partner, Johnson came to recognize his own responsibility by having unprotected sex. He told a group of Chicago-area teens, "You are the only person who can say, 'No, stop.'"[2]

The Simple Facts of Prevention

Most prevention efforts are focused on sex and drug habits. In general, prevention advice is, "Do not have sex, but if you do, use condoms; do not shoot drugs, but if you do, do not share needles." Those rules apply to everyone of both sexes except for uninfected partners in a relationship in which both partners are definitely uninfected, monogamous (having

Safer Sex Misunderstood

Many people do not follow safer-sex advice or do not understand it. In one study, nearly nine out of ten people said they were very sure or somewhat sure they knew how to put on a condom correctly. Yet when they demonstrated their ability on a penile model, only six in ten were able to do so.[3] In another study, only 36 percent of 646 sexually active people (average age 25 years; 83 percent of whom had never married) reported having safer sex with their most recent sex partner. Yet more than half of those were wrong; they did not use condoms! That study also found that less than a quarter of the people in the study ever asked his or her partner about whether he or she might have HIV. Less than half asked his or her partner if he or she used injection drugs.[4]

only one sex partner), and not drug users who share needles with others.

Except for such individuals, abstinence from sex is the only certain way not to get HIV through sex, but safer sex vastly reduces the risk. Safer sex means properly using a latex condom every time a man or woman has sex. The condom must be placed on the penis correctly, before any sexual contact is made, and kept in place until after the penis is removed from the vagina or rectum. Safer sex also means not sharing other body fluids, such as those passed in unprotected oral sex and possibly deep kissing.

People injecting drugs can prevent HIV infection by

always using a sterile needle, syringe, and works. That means no needle-sharing. In 1995, officials issued new guidelines on how to disinfect used needles: Addicts need to wash their works with soapy water, pull full-strength household bleach up into the syringe and keep it in there for thirty seconds, then rinse well before reuse.

Meanwhile, scientists have found the first known way to reduce HIV transmission from pregnant women to their babies. The reduction is achieved by giving pregnant women the antiviral drug AZT and then giving the drug to their newborns for six weeks. That approach reduced the incidence of HIV infection in newborns by two thirds. Although the long-term effects of AZT on the babies' development have not been determined, there were no serious short-term side effects for the babies or their mothers.[5]

Barriers to Prevention

Getting people to behave in safe ways, however, is not easy. Researcher Jeff Stryker and others noted the problems:

> Behavior modification is the single most important factor in HIV prevention, and the prevention efforts of the past decade have yielded a wealth of information both on the behavior of those at risk and the most successful forms of intervention [actions taken to change the behaviors]. Barriers to effective risk reduction include funding issues, impossible-to-meet expectations . . . cultural barriers and the belief that people will alter behavior simply because they know it is dangerous.[6]

How to Use a Condom

Although condoms are not perfect, they greatly reduce the chance for infection from HIV and several other sexually transmitted diseases. Here are some tips for the correct use of condoms.

- Always use latex condoms. Viruses are small enough to pass through animal skin condoms.
- Put the condom on as soon as the penis is erect and before any sexual contact is made.
- Place the condom on the end of the penis, leaving at least a one-half-inch space at the end of the condom. Pinch the end to remove any air. The rolled edge of the condom should be on the outside of the condom when placed on the penis.
- Gently unroll the condom to its full length.
- Leave the condom in place until the penis has been removed from the other person's body. Hold the condom in place when withdrawing it from the other person's body.
- Using a water-based lubricant, such as K-Y lubricating jelly, can help preserve a condom. Do not use oil-based lubricants such as Vaseline petroleum jelly or body lotion, because these can break down latex.
- Use a new condom for each act of vaginal, oral, or anal sex.

It is also important to be aware of your own and your partner's physical condition. Do not engage in sexual activity with or without a condom if either partner has any cuts, sores, or skin irritation.

Alas, people have shown time and again that they do not act in ways they know to be safe, as drunken driving statistics, for example, illustrate. In addition, the cultural barriers against prevention, such as peer pressure, are especially strong in groups whose infection rates are rising fastest. Those groups include young people and injection drug users, and within those groups, minority youth and women. In February 1996, the White House Office of National AIDS Policy issued a report noting that one in every four people who becomes infected in the United States is under the age of twenty.

Peer pressure, or the expectations of one's friends, among young people contributes to the spread of disease. For example, many teens feel that they need to have a boyfriend or girlfriend and that sex is an important and necessary part of that relationship. Some girls feel that they have to have sex to maintain the relationship. As one teen said, "Sex is just out there. If you won't do it, he will find somebody else who will."[7]

Those feelings are compounded by women's and girls' feelings of powerlessness where condom use is concerned.[8] Many men resist using condoms because they claim that doing so will reduce their sexual pleasure. One survey of African-American and Hispanic women found that the women did not ask their partners to use condoms because they did not think their sex partners had AIDS, they did not know where to get or how to use condoms, or they were uncomfortable talking about condoms with their partners.[9]

Preventive Therapies

Advances in HIV treatments have created a demand for preventive antiviral drug therapies. Patients are asking their doctors for the drug therapy after they have had unprotected sex or believe they have been exposed in other ways to HIV. Some physicians are complying with the requests, but AIDS experts have numerous concerns about it. Besides the usual concerns for such therapy (expense, side effects), they note there is no proof that the therapy works. Also, they worry that widespread use could hinder other prevention efforts and encourage the development of drug-resistant HIV.[10]

Women and girls can improve their situation by learning more. First, they can learn how to negotiate safer sex. To do so, they can keep their own supply of condoms. They can suggest making the condom part of the sexual experience by offering to place the condom on their partner's penis. Another possibility includes getting and using female condoms. When these efforts fail, young women need to know the choice may be between losing a boyfriend and losing their lives.

Teens also put themselves at risk because they think AIDS cannot happen to them. One young woman kept having unprotected sex even after being warned that her healthy-seeming boyfriend was infected. She, too, became infected. A young man who knew he could get AIDS by having sex without a condom did it anyway, with women and with men. He said, "I didn't worry about it. I thought I was invincible."[11] His HIV test proved him wrong.

Peer pressure can be used to improve prevention efforts. Researchers have found that people are more likely to change their behavior if safe practices are perceived as the in thing to do.[12] If someone feels that "everyone else" is using condoms, for example, then that person is much more likely to use condoms.[13] Knowing exactly what to do and how to do it, and getting support from one's friends, also helps people behave safely. Thus, when teenagers tell other teens to use condoms, teens are more likely to use them. The same thing is true for drug users. Prevention messages need to address their audience in the audience's own language. Repetition and ongoing support for the message also help.[14]

Changing behaviors among IV drug users is difficult because of the culture in which they live. Sharing needles, for example, is sometimes a ritual among users. The drugs themselves can undermine users' judgment. Women drug users said they did not clean their needles because they had to use friends' needles, were high on drugs and not interested in cleaning needles, or did not have disinfectant available.[15] A person under the influence of injected drugs may make bad decisions not only about needle-sharing, but also about sex. Some drug addicts, especially women, trade sex for drugs, and

Another prevention message from the U.S. Centers for Disease Control and Prevention reads "There's a simple way to prevent AIDS . . . Don't have sex. And as long as you aren't shooting drugs, you'll be fine."

addicts who are desperate for drugs may not demand that their partners use condoms.

Politics adds another barrier to prevention. Local, state, and federal politicians fear that spending money to provide clean needles to addicts or to provide condoms to sexually active teens will appear to endorse drug use and teen sex. In fact, the United States Congress enacted a law prohibiting federal funds to be spent on providing clean needles to addicts.[16] Similarly, suggestions to make condoms available at high schools have caused uproars at school board meetings across the country. As a result, few schools have allowed condom distribution. Government-produced advertisements promoting condom use have been criticized as encouraging people to have multiple sex partners.[17]

A survey has found that the American people support such preventive actions, however. The Kaiser Family Foundation Survey on Americans and AIDS/HIV found in March 1996 that 72 percent of adults surveyed favored condom ads on network television. Also, 66 percent of those surveyed favored providing clean needles to IV drug users. Support was evenly split between providing condoms in high schools and providing only information about HIV and AIDS.[18]

Prevention in Practice: Needle Exchange Programs

One much-debated way to get drug users to use sterile needles is called a needle exchange program. Such programs typically provide a drug addict with sterile needles in exchange for a used set. The intention is to remove potential HIV sources from the streets and, thereby, reduce the spread of HIV. Since about one third of all AIDS cases are related to IV drug use, reducing infection sources is very important to reducing AIDS transmission. The law that Congress enacted in 1988 prohibiting federal spending for needle exchange programs allows the ban to be lifted if "the Surgeon General determines that such programs are effective in preventing the spread of HIV and do not encourage the use of illegal drugs."[19]

As it turns out, needle exchange programs (funded by private and local sources) have been successful. A study sponsored by the CDC and led by Dr. Peter Lurie of the University of California at San Francisco found that addicts in seventy needle exchange programs shared needles less and injected drugs less often than other addicts. Other studies have found that users involved in needle exchange programs were more likely to seek treatment.[20] Needle sharing dropped by 40 percent

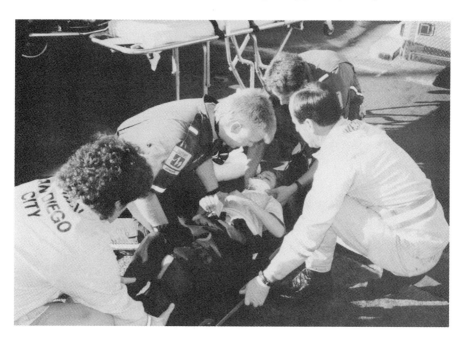

Blood at an accident scene may be contaminated with HIV, so emergency medical workers must take measures to prevent possible infection.

among drug users in Connecticut after the state passed a law in 1992 that allowed pharmacies to sell needles without a prescription.[21] In September 1995, a panel of experts brought together by the National Academy of Sciences found that needle exchange programs greatly reduced the spread of HIV without increasing drug use.[22]

National political institutions have not responded to those reports. The Foundation for Drug Policy, a group in Washington, D.C., set out in 1995 to gather more support for ending the ban on federal funding for needle programs. In April 1998, the administration of President Bill Clinton endorsed needle exchange programs as effective in reducing the spread of AIDS. However, the administration left the funding ban in place.[23]

Prevention in Practice: Condom Information and Distribution

Efforts to publicize the importance of condom use have met with similar frustrations. Newspapers, magazines, and television stations generally decline to run commercial advertising that promotes condoms. Schools, which perhaps have the greatest opportunity to teach young people about condoms, frequently are limited in what they may say about HIV transmission.[24] Most schools have bowed to opponents who fear that teaching about condom use will encourage teens to have sex.

Concerns about the possibility of AIDS information promoting sex, however, appear to be misplaced. A report on prevention programs by researcher David R. Holtgrave and others says flatly, "The discussion of HIV-related issues in schools does not spur the onset of sexual activity among youth."[25] The report also took note of a successful condom advertising campaign:

> Since 1986, Switzerland has supported broad-based social marketing of condoms to curb the transmission of HIV infection, particularly among adolescents and young adults. From 1987 to 1990, this active promotion of condom use neither significantly increased the proportion of adolescents engaging in sexual intercourse nor the average number of sexual partners, but it did increase reported condom use markedly. Among young adults engaging in casual sex, the proportion using condoms every time also significantly increased. These results suggest important lessons . . . for HIV prevention efforts in the United States.[26]

Nevertheless, condom advertisements continue to be mostly absent from United States television and newspapers. In January 1994, the CDC and Health and Human Services announced an advertising campaign aimed at slowing the spread of HIV and other sexually transmitted diseases. The campaign of nine television and four radio ads was aimed at people ages eighteen to twenty-five and promoted abstinence and using latex condoms.[27]

Knowledge into Action

Nowadays, thanks to public education programs and news media, most people know how a person gets AIDS. Knowledge, however, has not translated into action. HIV is most prevalent among gay men, and older gay men largely have changed their behaviors. However, a CDC survey released in February 1996 indicates that many young homosexual men are still having unprotected sex. The survey of gay men ages fifteen to twenty-two found that 38 percent reported unprotected anal sex in the preceding six months.[28]

The Cost of Prevention

The cost of prevention, meanwhile, is high and hard to measure, but it is not nearly as high as the cost of caring for an AIDS patient. It also is not nearly as high as the cost to society of losing the lives and talents of hundreds of thousands more people. The Holtgrave report on prevention concluded, "Although it is difficult to state precisely the exact effect of an HIV prevention program . . . it is relatively easy to demonstrate that, even if the favorable impact is quite small, the [prevention] program can yield net economic benefits to society." Thus, efforts to change people's behavior for the sake of AIDS prevention are sure to continue.[29]

7

Social Implications

The impact of AIDS goes beyond health. AIDS has affected sexual behaviors and magnified issues involving prejudice, poverty, and individual rights. These issues have come into play in determining who gets tested for AIDS and what is done with results; in deciding how research money is spent; and in day-to-day living for millions of people.

Darren Sack, a hemophiliac, learned firsthand about prejudice and individual rights. Sack contracted HIV from the injections of clotting factor he took to make his blood coagulate. When a newspaper ran a story about him, the owner of the Burger King where Sack worked fired him. Sack and his family fought his dismissal. "Eventually I got taken back, and he [the owner] made my life miserable," Sack recalled. "But I stayed another seven, eight months just to show him." At his school, a group of students staged a walkout to protest Sack's attendance during his junior year of high school. Some students refused to sit by him. His junior prom date's parents made her cancel after they realized Sack had HIV. "The problem is that HIV has such a social stigma attached to it," Sack said. "As a result, people push you away or avoid you instead of being sympathetic."[1]

Sack's experience is not unusual. An associate pastor in Colorado lost his job because his wife and two children were infected.[2] In the early days of the epidemic, medical personnel refused to treat AIDS patients. Landlords refused to rent to them. Soon, laws were passed that forbade such discrimination. Those laws, and increased knowledge of AIDS, have reduced discrimination. Still, prejudice is a shadow never far from AIDS discussions.

Public and Individual Rights

Fear, prejudice, and individual rights came into play when the HIV antibody test became widely available. The nation debated the questions of who should be tested and what should be done with the results. Some people called for universal testing, but that idea was abandoned as impractical, ineffective, and an invasion of privacy. At that time, blood banks and special sites set up for HIV testing immediately began using the test for people who wanted it. Blood donors were required to be tested, but some people argued for mandatory testing of other groups. They said that in an epidemic, public health concerns override individual rights to privacy. People promoting individual rights argued that any

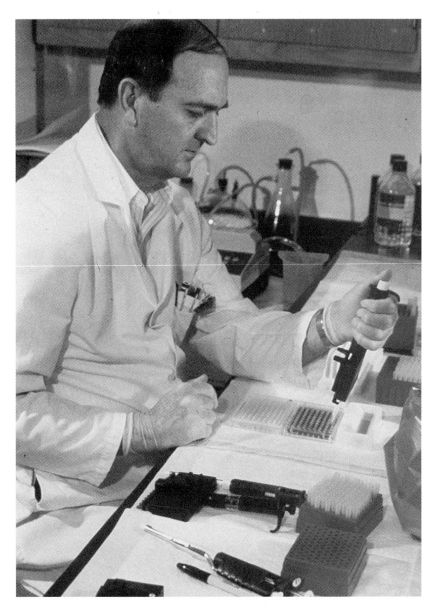

A researcher performs standard enzyme linked immunosorbent assay (ELISA), using samples of dried blood on filter paper. All blood donors are required to be tested for HIV.

tests be voluntary and anonymous—meaning no one would be required to be tested, and no one would be able to link test results to any particular individual. Tests have remained voluntary except for in a few groups, such as new military recruits. Whether tests are anonymous depends on state laws.

The question of who should be tested relates closely to the issue of whether test results would be reported to public health authorities. Medical personnel are required to report occurrences of certain diseases to state public health officials to help them keep track of epidemics. Reportable diseases include tuberculosis and such sexually transmitted diseases as syphilis, gonorrhea, and AIDS (but not earlier stages of HIV infection).

Soon after HIV antibody testing started, states began to propose that doctors and clinics report cases of HIV infection to public health authorities. Public health officials wanted the information so that they could track the epidemic better. Opposition was fierce. Civil rights groups said reporting would scare people away from being tested and, as a result, provide no public benefit. The question of reporting also tied into the question of confidential versus anonymous testing. With confidential testing (and reporting), names would be linked to test results but would be kept private. Confidential reporting would allow epidemiologists to weed out duplicates and possibly link one year's HIV infections with another year's AIDS cases. With anonymous testing, each individual test would be identified only by a number or some similar identification. Anonymous reporting, as a result, would not permit matching of infections with AIDS or eliminating duplicates.

Eventually, the CDC suggested only that state departments of health consider mandatory reporting.

States adopted a variety of reporting requirements. As of 1996, twenty-four states required confidential testing and reporting of HIV infection. Several others required reporting of test results but not the names of the people being tested. This method allows states to keep track of the number and location of infected people. Several others have no reporting requirements. Marc Vargo, author of *The HIV Test*, writes,

> Many citizens would not seek an HIV assessment if they knew that their names and test findings would be forwarded to a government health department, and it is for this reason that many states do not require the reporting of such information. Further, even those that do mandate the reporting of names sometimes provide the means by which a person may undergo anonymous testing.[3]

Some states, for example, ask for names but do not require identification. Thus, use of false names is widespread.

Similarly, some states have active programs for tracing contacts, and some do not. Contact tracing is the practice of health officials' finding persons who may have come into contact with an infected person and recommending testing. Opponents see contact tracing as another threat to privacy. Other people see contact tracing as a very useful way to track the epidemic and to prevent its further spread. A handful of studies have found that contact tracing effectively locates previously undiagnosed infections. When the contacted persons learn of their infections, they tend to take precautions that help prevent further infections through sex or pregnancy.

Although contact tracing requires a lot of work, it could provide long-term savings since it would stop some new infections. The money saved by preventing new infections would more than make up for the cost of the contact tracing. Nevertheless, civil liberties groups have vigorously opposed contact tracing—even when voluntary—as another opportunity for unscrupulous or uncaring public officials to know the names of infected people.

After bitter fights in states where contact tracing was proposed, an organization of state health officers recommended

Individual states have adopted different reporting requirements for HIV test results.

that each state encourage some form of contact notification. In time, many state and local officials discovered that some infected individuals wanted help in notifying their sex or needle-sharing contacts. As a result, health officials generally try to make available contact tracing or some other partner notification program if an infected person asks for help.

Spreading the Word

Most observers believe that improved public knowledge will not only help slow the epidemic but will also reduce discrimination. Numerous HIV-positive people across America have demonstrated their commitment to that idea by becoming vocal advocates for AIDS education. Basketball superstar Earvin "Magic" Johnson set an example in speaking out about AIDS. Others far less famous have followed suit in their communities. One of them, Pedro Zamora, became a beloved friend to MTV viewers. Zamora, after learning about his infection, worked hard in Florida to inform people about AIDS. Then he applied to be a participant on MTV's show *The Real World.* That show puts people together as roommates and videotapes their real lives. Zamora moved to San Francisco to became one of those people. Zamora, who contracted HIV through unprotected sex, died in November 1994 at the age of twenty-two. He is credited with putting a face on the AIDS epidemic.

In most ways, Zamora was no different from many other Americans. He did, however, have a couple of characteristics that made him more typical of AIDS sufferers than of the general population. Zamora, who was born in Cuba, was Hispanic, and he was gay. Those two characteristics made him a minority. Historically, minorities in any culture have experienced discrimination.

Discrimination Around the World

Worldwide, the AIDS epidemic mostly affects people who already suffer the ravages of poverty and discrimination. Thus, AIDS in the United States and other industrialized countries is largely a disease of racial and ethnic minorities and of homosexuals. By the same token, AIDS worldwide is largely a disease of impoverished nations. Within those nations, the people most impoverished and discriminated against are the most common victims.

AIDS is devastating in the developing world. The World Health Organization (WHO) estimated that more than 11.7 million people worldwide had died of AIDS and related causes by December 1997. The United Nations' AIDS organization (UNAIDS) estimated that 5.8 million people were newly infected with HIV in 1997, and 30.6 million were living with HIV infection or AIDS.[4] Every region of the world, except for Antarctica, has been struck.

Governmental responses to AIDS and HIV have been universally slow. Governments worldwide initially dealt with the epidemic by ignoring or minimizing the impact of AIDS. They were slow to enforce strict screening programs for the blood supply and, some people charge, failed to respond to the epidemic because it affected people who were poor, homosexual, or nonwhite. Now that the infection is indeed a widespread epidemic, or pandemic, governments and health officials are working to develop strategies to stop the spread of HIV.

Discrimination and the Epidemic

Poverty has contributed to the HIV pandemic in several ways. Generally, people who are poor have less access to health care. They also are more likely to be illiterate and less likely to be aware of preventive measures. Poor people are more likely to live in cramped conditions that breed infection. Thus, they are

HIV Around the World

Two thirds of all people living with HIV infections are in sub-Saharan Africa.[5] One forecast estimates that AIDS will double the death rate in thirteen African countries by 2010.[6] In the southern African nation of Malawi, the AIDS death toll is expected to cause the average life span to decrease from fifty-seven years to thirty-three years. In Uganda, AIDS causes 50 percent of all deaths and 90 percent of deaths among people under thirty-five years old.[7] The World Health Organization estimates almost one in five adults are infected in Botswana, Zambia, and Zimbabwe. The number of infections in Southeast Asia is soaring; rates in Thailand increased ten times between 1990 and 1994.[8] Yet rates are fairly low and stable in a few countries in Africa, lending hope that the African epidemic can be stabilized.[9]

more susceptible to opportunistic infections that may cause them to die sooner when they have HIV infection. Also, poor people are often overlooked for new treatments or vaccines. That is because poor people cannot pay the high costs of treatment.

The United States and other developed nations—the relatively wealthy countries—have concentrated their resources on their infections at home. The reason is money. Manufacturers know that although about 90 percent of HIV infections is in developing nations, those nations do not have money to spend on drugs or vaccines. For example, although AZT can cut HIV transmission from pregnant women to babies by two thirds, young African women do not have easy access to this drug. Cost may prohibit its use in poorer countries.[10]

Some of the world's population uses traditional medicines rather than modern medical doctors and drugs. Traditional healers use herbal preparations, acupuncture, and other readily available, low-cost treatments. For AIDS sufferers throughout most of the world, the drugs of scientific advances simply are not available because of the cost. An organization called the Center for Natural and Traditional Medicines is attempting to coordinate HIV and AIDS research efforts in traditional medicine. But the center, which is headquartered in Washington, D.C., has been frustrated in its efforts to get funding for research.[11]

Developed nations do provide a large share of the funding for international efforts such as the WHO. The amounts of money needed are immense. An official with WHO estimated in 1994 that it needed about $2.5 billion just to implement prevention programs in developing countries.

Research Aims at Developed Countries

Meanwhile, most research involves HIV-1, subtype B, which is the most common type of HIV in North America and Europe. Other subtypes are more common in Africa and Asia. Researchers feel that developed countries' research must consider the other subtypes.

For example, in Thailand, subtype E seems to move faster than subtype B. It may not be long before subtype E travels across borders and oceans to cause serious problems among heterosexuals in the United States and Europe.[12]

A move to investigate other subtypes is developing. Subtype E, most common in Asia, was found in five soldiers from Uruguay who had served in Cambodia. Some experimental studies indicate that subtype E appears to be significantly more contagious by sexual intercourse than subtype B. Some cases of subtype F have been identified in Brazil. In addition, subtypes A, D, and E were found in five United States military men who had served overseas. Also, an African student in the United States had subtype D, acquired before entering the United States.

In 1995, the Centers for Disease Control reported that two cases of HIV-2 infection had been detected in donated blood. HIV-2 is a variant of HIV, or HIV-1. HIV-2 may be somewhat milder than HIV-1 in terms of decreased CD4 count. HIV-2 still causes AIDS, although it may take longer to develop. HIV-2 is most commonly spread through heterosexual contact. Blood centers in the United States began screening for HIV-2 in June 1992. As of June 1995, HIV-2 infection had been identified in sixty-two people in the United States. Most of these people were from western Africa and others of them had traveled to western Africa or had had sex with someone from western Africa.[13]

Prevention and Culture

Most HIV infections outside the United States and Europe are transmitted through heterosexual contact. Therefore, attitudes

HIV-2 is spread mostly through heterosexual contact.

about men and women and their sex roles affect prevention education.

In Africa, most of the infected women have one sex part-ner—their husbands—who hold the power in their relationship. The husbands, however, usually have more than one sex partner, as is the tradition. Even if the wives know they and their unborn children are at risk of infection, the wives often do not have enough power in the relationship to demand that their husbands use condoms.[14] To prevent the spread of disease in Africa, then, requires improving women's standing in society. "Up until now, you really couldn't say 'condom' in Africa," says Judith Senderowitz, a reproductive-health consultant to the United Nations. "Now, thanks to AIDS, you can."[15]

8

The Future of AIDS

Many scientists agree that the best long-term solution to AIDS is a vaccine. Although treatments have extended patients' lives, no one has been cured or is expected to be cured for now. Also, education as a means of prevention has had only small effects on reducing people's risky behavior. AIDS treatments, meanwhile, often run into the tens of thousands of dollars per person, whereas a vaccine might cost around one hundred dollars.

Problems in the Vaccine Hunt

Finding a vaccine, however, has been a frustrating exercise with numerous problems. First among these is HIV's tendency to mutate. Fears about vaccine safety are another issue to be resolved. In addition, politics and funding problems have affected the search for a vaccine.[1] In the United States, only about 10 percent of the government's $1.5 billion AIDS research budget goes to vaccines.[2] Wayne C. Koff, a pharmaceutical company executive, argues that financial incentives are needed to change that situation, because manufacturers do not think they can make money by producing a vaccine.[3]

While manufacturers foresee little profit in successful vaccines, they see great possibilities for financial losses if they are less than totally successful. They worry about being held responsible for infections that might arise after vaccines are administered. Koff argues for several public policy steps to encourage companies to develop preventive vaccines. His suggestions include tax incentives for vaccine development, government guarantees to purchase an approved vaccine, and exclusion of AIDS vaccines from any government price control laws.[4]

Vaccine researchers took heart in 1997, though, when President Bill Clinton challenged them to develop a vaccine within ten years[5] and the National Institutes of Health established a new AIDS vaccine research center.

What We Know Now

Scientists know that a person's body can have germ-stopping antibodies to HIV but still not disable the virus. They have learned, in fact, that the body produces large volumes of antibodies. HIV reproduces and changes so quickly, though, that the virus outpaces the antibodies' ability to stop the virus or to adapt to the mutated virus.

Scientists have identified the protein gp120 on HIV's surface that the antibodies are attracted to. Gp120 also is important in allowing the virus to fasten itself to CD4 cells. Scientists have been able to artificially produce the gp120 protein.[6]

In addition, government scientists announced in May 1996 the discovery of a protein they named fusin, now known as CXCR4. The protein is essential to HIV's ability to enter CD4 cells after the virus attaches to the cells. The discovery is considered a major advance and is expected to help in the search for an effective vaccine. More recently, another co-receptor used by many more HIV strains was discovered. It is known as CCR5.[7]

Studying Survivors

Researchers have learned more by studying long-term nonprogressors. These people are infected with the virus but have not developed any AIDS-related symptoms. The HIV in one group of long-term nonprogressors was found to be missing parts of a gene called *nef*, which appears to be important to HIV reproduction.[8] In this group, people have HIV antibodies and other immune activities that seem to keep up with HIV reproduction. (Both long-term nonprogressors and AIDS patients have HIV antibodies. In AIDS patients, however, HIV reproduces faster than the antibodies can disable the virus.) In 1997, another mutated gene, that for the CCR5 co-receptor, was identified in long-term nonprogressors.[9]

President Bill Clinton challenged vaccine researchers to develop an AIDS vaccine by the year 2007.

Search for Natural Immunity

Other small groups of people have provided researchers with interesting bits of information, or at least other ideas to study. One of these is a small group of women prostitutes in Gambia, a nation in Africa. Scientist Sarah Rowland-Jones and others reported in 1995 that five of six women studied remain uninfected by HIV despite repeated exposure to the most common HIV strains in the region. The five women had no detectable virus or antibodies.[10]

Researchers exposed disease-fighting cells from the women to cells with HIV proteins. The disease-fighters immediately killed the cells with the HIV proteins. That activity indicated that the women's immune systems were familiar with HIV. The researchers suspect that the women may have been exposed previously to a very weak form of HIV or HIV in a very low dosage. That weak exposure may have allowed the women's immune systems to clear, or eliminate, the HIV infection. Their immune systems then were prepared to knock down any further exposures to HIV, just as a person who has had mumps is able to ward off later mumps infections. If that is so, the women have developed a natural immunity to later HIV infections. Since the existence of a natural immunity is considered critical to knowing that a vaccine is possible, this news is very exciting for researchers.

A child in California also has provided evidence of a natural immune response. A kindergarten boy appeared to have cleared the virus from his system. This child had tested positive for HIV when he was nineteen days old and again a month later. However, tests could find no signs of the virus four years later, although tests indicated that the boy had been actively infected. It is still unclear whether the child's CD4 cells were totally infected or whether some maternal cells that had been carrying the virus were cleared. Other cases had been reported of babies who appeared to have cleared HIV from their systems, but this case was the best documented.[11]

Another group of people appears to be at least partially immune to HIV, or, more specifically, to HIV-1, the virus responsible for most of the world's AIDS. This group of people is infected with HIV-2, the weaker cousin to HIV-1 that is found almost exclusively in western Africa. Researchers found that this group was less likely to contract HIV-1. Perhaps the HIV-2 provided protection from HIV-1. The most convincing data on people with resistance to HIV infection are people with two mutant genes for the CCR5 co-receptor.

Studies Under Way

Vaccine researchers, with the help of these studies, have developed or are working on vaccines to disable HIV by standard vaccine methods. One method alters live HIV viruses (called attenuated viruses). Another inactivates whole HIV viruses. In a third method, viruses that do not cause disease are altered so that they cause an immune response to HIV. About fifteen vaccines to protect people from HIV viruses are being studied in the United States. About fifteen therapeutic vaccines are also being studied. A therapeutic vaccine tries to stop the advance of an existing HIV infection rather than prevent an initial infection.

Scientists are using the tools of contemporary technology to develop vaccines based on HIV surface proteins and vaccines based on DNA. Vaccines based on the gp120 protein on the HIV virus are intended to prime a person's immune system to recognize the protein on HIV as an invader. The idea is that when a person is later exposed to HIV, his or her body will be able to respond instantly and kill the virus. The body could respond because it will have made antibodies to the gp120 protein. A DNA vaccine works in a similar way. With a DNA vaccine, the genetic code for HIV proteins is injected into the body. DNA vaccines seem to cause a stronger and longer-lasting immune response than do vaccines based on the proteins themselves.

Animal Models

Among the scientific difficulties, however, is the absence of a good animal model for testing vaccines, although one is being tried. Chimpanzees—humans' closest genetic cousin—can become infected with HIV, but they usually do not develop AIDS. Another mammal, the macaque monkey, develops AIDS, but the condition is caused not by HIV; it is caused by a viral cousin, simian immunodeficiency virus (SIV). Therefore, tests on macaques must be based on SIV, and the results are not directly applicable to humans. Just the same, some SIV vaccines have been tested on the monkeys. Those vaccines have been very successful in preventing infection. Unfortunately, however, the vaccine caused illness and death in some newborn monkeys. That problem raised fears that attenuated viruses might do the same in human beings.[12]

Adding to the vaccine development difficulties is the fact that HIV-1 has at least nine subtypes. Scientists worry that a vaccine that creates immunity against one subtype might not create immunity against all the others. Many researchers feel strongly that multiple approaches are needed to create immunity against HIV, but those approaches are not currently being made.

Trials Planned

Primary concern, of course, is that any vaccine tested in human trials is both safe and effective. That concern caused the cancellation of trials in the United States. Two experimental vaccines using gp120 products had been scheduled for phase-three human trials in the United States. Phase-three trials are the ones attempting to prove the vaccines indeed work. Phase-one and -two trials had shown that the vaccines appear to be safe in the short run and might create immunity, although not nearly as well as was hoped. In 1994, the National Institute of Allergy and Infectious Diseases (NIAID), which is overseeing much AIDS research, canceled the rest of the trials.[13] Officials at the agency thought the vaccine had not been effective enough to proceed. The decision not to do phase-three trials was criticized by many scientists, who believe the need is so urgent that the possibility of a vaccine that immunized only some of the recipients still would be valuable. Dr. Jose Esparza of the World Health

Organization Global Programme on AIDS stated that the experimental vaccines, developed by two American companies, "do have merit and deserve to be tested" in phase-three trials. He believed that the vaccines "may work, and we may be missing precious time by not testing them." If the vaccines do not work, he said, "we had better know that now, so that new approaches to development are explored."[14]

In 1998, the first large-scale human trials were expected to begin in Thailand and the United States. These trials of a gp120-based vaccine were to be conducted by a biotechnology company called VaxGen. The United States government will not fund such trials because of concerns about the vaccine's effectiveness. As a result, California-based VaxGen was raising $20 million in private funds to pay for the trials. The trials were expected to include five thousand volunteers in the United States and twenty-five hundred in Thailand. The vaccines to be tested will include two types of gp120. One type will be from a previously tested laboratory strain. The other type will be from HIV strains circulating in the United States or Thailand, depending on where the vaccines will be tested.

Such testing remains controversial. Still, vaccine expert Mary Lou Clements-Mann, a member of the Food and Drug Administration's vaccine advisory committee, said that phase-three trials are important. "If we don't move forward to phase three, we will never have a vaccine," she said.[15]

Meanwhile, in early 1996 the Food and Drug Administration gave researchers permission to try the first ever DNA vaccine on humans. Researchers from the University of

Pennsylvania and a biotechnology company called Apollon began the trial with HIV-positive people in 1996. This trial is testing the safety of injecting pure DNA for HIV proteins. DNA does not survive long in the bloodstream, but researchers want to make sure it does not somehow make its way into humans' own gene systems.

Ethics and Vaccines

Ethical questions also dog vaccine testing efforts. These questions involve that old problem, human behavior. Trial participants need to realize that the vaccines are experimental and may not provide protection against HIV. They must also understand that they may receive a placebo, which is an inactive substance. Unfortunately, people in such trials time and again have tended to ignore such warnings from researchers and behave as if the experimental vaccine is certain to provide immunity.[16]

One ethics expert thinks independent groups should deliver the safety message to participants, since researchers have conflicting goals in explaining a trial. While the researchers in their hearts may want the participants to behave safely, they know in their heads that their studies will be more meaningful if participants indeed behave in unsafe ways.

Some people question whether it is ethical to test vaccines, such as those based on gp120, in a developing country like Thailand when United States government officials decline to sponsor tests of the vaccines at home. Others argue the other side: It is unethical to withhold a possible vaccine from countries where infection rates are high.[17]

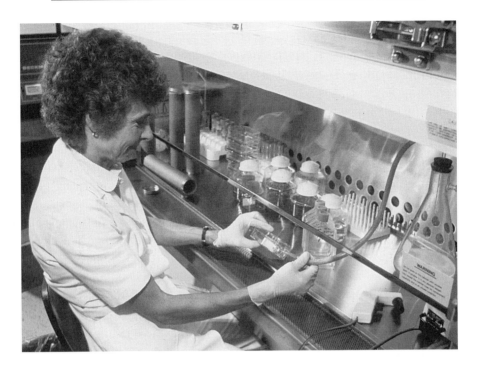

Researchers are working to develop a vaccine for AIDS, as well as more effective treatments for HIV.

Another dilemma is what to do about the vaccine trial participants who are not infected with AIDS but, because of the vaccines, have HIV antibodies in their blood. Since most HIV tests screen for antibodies (rather than for actual infection), these people would appear as HIV-positive in blood tests. Ideas have been tried, with some success, to provide special identification cards to participants. Those cards would explain the person's test participation to an insurance company or employer and provide a telephone number the companies could call to confirm the information.

The problems of money and safety will continue to create stumbling blocks for vaccine researchers. Each new piece of information, though, adds to hopes that a vaccine will be found that provides at least some protection.

Treatment Research

Scientists, meanwhile, continue to search for more effective treatments for HIV. One study announced in 1995 found that HIV patients may benefit from intermittently taking interleukin-2. Interleukin-2, which the body produces naturally, gives a boost to the body's immune system.[18] Also in 1995, preliminary tests of an anticancer compound called hydroxyurea showed potential for HIV suppression. Hydroxyurea depletes cells of an enzyme necessary for HIV replication.[19]

In February 1996, the FDA decided to let a company move ahead with trials on a controversial treatment sometimes called hyperthermia. In it, a patient's blood is removed, heated to 114 degrees Fahrenheit, and then returned to the body. Theory has it that the heating kills enough of the virus to allow a patient's immune system to recover enough to extend the patient's life. The theory is widely disputed by many scientists, but initial tests have found it to be safe.[20]

Prevention Research

Combining condoms with substances that kill HIV is being investigated as a safer approach to sex. Officials used to recommend nonoxynol-9, a common spermicide (a sperm-killing agent used in contraceptive foams and in other external contraceptives) that also kills HIV in sperm. Concern about nonoxynol-9 causing irritation and capillary breakage arose. Nonoxynol-9 alone, without a condom, is no longer generally recommended. Researchers are taking a new look at nonoxynol-9 used in low dosages as a preventive measure. They also are studying at least two other substances that women could use vaginally to prevent HIV infection.[21]

Looking Ahead

Scientists continue to puzzle over vaccines, treatments, and preventions. Much progress has been made, but much work remains. Until a cure or vaccine has been found, unprotected sex will continue to be a high-risk venture around the world.

Q & A

Q. Are AIDS and HIV infection the same thing?

A. No, but they certainly are related. *HIV* stands for *human immunodeficiency virus*. It is a retrovirus that attacks CD4-positive T cells, an important part of the human immune system. People who are infected with HIV thus have damaged immune systems. AIDS is essentially the final stage of HIV infection. When a person has AIDS, the HIV infection has advanced so far that few CD4 cells remain, and the person experiences various opportunistic infections or tumors. Opportunistic infections and tumors are diseases and cancers that rarely occur in people with healthy immune systems.

Q. Now that AIDS patients are having success with the three-drug antiviral treatments, can people stop worrying about AIDS and HIV?

A. No. Although those treatments are a major breakthrough, several problems exist. First, no one knows for how long the drugs will suppress HIV, since HIV has always developed resistance to other treatments. Second, even when HIV counts drop dramatically, the virus can still be passed to another person. Third, the treatments are so expensive that many, many infected persons cannot afford to get them.

Q. How can I tell if someone has HIV infection?

A. You probably cannot. During many years of HIV infection, most people show no outward signs of being infected. During a period known as AIDS-wasting syndrome, however, an infected person may look very ill, since he or she may lose a lot of weight, sleep poorly, and have diarrhea. Once the infection has advanced to AIDS, a person's appearance will depend on what opportunistic infections and growths affect him or her.

Q. Is it really necessary for doctors, dentists, and nurses to wear masks and rubber gloves, and so on, when they are treating people?

A. Yes, it is. As previously noted, no one—including medical personnel—can tell just by looking whether a person is infected. As a result, anyone dealing with blood or other body fluids must take the same precautions as he or she would if infection were apparent. Besides, HIV is not the only life-threatening blood-borne microbe. People who wear masks and gloves when they may be exposed to blood and other body fluids are not going overboard; they are being smart.

Q. If somebody at school has AIDS, how should I act? How can I protect myself?

A. Try being a friend. Like anyone else, a person with AIDS wants to have friends and have fun. His or her activities, however, may be restricted because of the illness. You need not be afraid of "catching" AIDS as long as you practice the basic rules of avoiding HIV infection: Do not have sex or share needles with the infected person. It is also a good idea not to share razors or toothbrushes or engage in deep kissing.

Q. I am worried I might have been exposed to HIV, since I just found out my boyfriend sometimes shoots drugs. What should I do?

A. First, make sure you do not have unprotected sex with your boyfriend (or anyone else). You may then want to call your county health department to inquire about getting tested. People there should be able to tell you the cost, the timing, and whether your test can be anonymous.

Q. What can a woman do to avoid HIV infection if her sex partner refuses to use a condom?

A. Most important, she can refuse to have sex. Meanwhile, scientists are testing several microbicides that would kill HIV vaginally. Also, a female condom has been tested and is available. In addition, a sexually active woman can make sure that she keeps condoms on hand in case her boyfriend forgets. A woman also can suggest other sexual activities that do not involve vaginal intercourse, anal intercourse, or oral sex.

AIDS Timeline

1969— A St. Louis teenager died mysteriously after overwhelming infections. The case later became the earliest documented AIDS death.

1979—One woman and two men were treated for AIDS-related diseases.

1981—Disease-control officials in the United States labeled AIDS a new medical syndrome in June after several individuals died from a set of rare diseases.

1982—U.S. Centers for Disease Control and Prevention declared an epidemic in September.

1983— A retrovirus, eventually called human immunodeficiency virus, or HIV, was identified as the cause of AIDS.

1984— A test to detect HIV antibodies was available to researchers.

1985— AZT was identified as a possible treatment for HIV infection.

1987— AZT was released for distribution to HIV and AIDS patients.

1996— A three-drug combination was found that drastically reduced the amount of HIV in the bloodstream of infected individuals.

1997—President Bill Clinton called for an HIV vaccine within ten years.

For More Information

American Foundation for AIDS Research (AmFAR)
733 Third Avenue, 12th Floor
New York, NY 10017
212-682-7440
AmFAR publishes the *AIDS/HIV Treatment Directory*, a biannual comprehensive guide to approved and experimental AIDS-related treatments and clinical trials.

CDC National AIDS Hotline
1-800-342-2437 (English, 24 hours a day)
1-800-344-7432 (Spanish, 8:00 A.M.–2:00 A.M. EST)
1-800-243-7889 (TTY for hearing impaired)

Gay Men's Health Crisis
119 West 24th Street
New York, NY 10011
1-212-807-6664 (offices)
1-212-807-6655 (hotline)
Internet: <http://www.gmhc.org>
Long-established nonprofit organization providing information, support, and advocacy.

National AIDS Clearinghouse
1-800-458-5231
Internet: <http://www.cdcnac.org/nachome.html>
Distributes government publications and has a variety of other information pertaining to HIV and AIDS. A wealth of information is available.

National Institute of Allergy and Infectious Diseases
National Institutes of Health
Bethesda, MD 20892
Internet: <http://www.niaid.nih.gov/>

Internet Resources

AEGIS, AIDS Education Global Information System
<http://www.aegis.com>

Centers for Disease Control
Division of HIV/AIDS Prevention
<http://www.cdc.gov/nchstp/hiv_aids/dhap.htm>

***Journal of the American Medical Association* HIV/AIDS Information Center**
<http://www.ama-assn.org/special/hiv/hivhome.htm>

National Library of Medicine
HIV/AIDS Resources
<http://sis.nlm.nih.gov/aidswww.htm>

UNAIDS, The Joint United Nations Programme on HIV/AIDS
<http://www.unaids.org/>

Usenet newsgroup: sci.med.aids
Monitored newsgroup.

Chapter Notes

Chapter 2. The History of AIDS

1. John Crewdson, "Case Shakes Theories of AIDS Origin," *Chicago Tribune*, October 25, 1987, p. 1

2. David Concar, "AIDS Epidemiology: Another Early Case Identified," *Nature*, vol. 346, July 12, 1990, p. 95.

3. Centers for Disease Control and Prevention, *HIV/AIDS Surveillance Report*, 1996, year-end edition, vol. 8, no. 2, p. 19.

4. Randy Shilts, *And the Band Played On: Politics, People and the AIDS Epidemic* (New York: St. Martin's Press), 1987, 1988, p. 54.

5. Ibid., p.72.

6. CDC, p. 19.

7. Shilts, p. 83.

8. Ibid., p. xxii.

9. Ibid., p. 177.

10. CDC, p. 19.

11. Peter S. Arno and Karyn L. Feiden, *Against the Odds: The Story of AIDS Drug Development, Politics and Profits* (New York: HarperCollins Publishers), 1992, p. 4.

12. Shilts, p. xxiii.

13. Centers for Disease Control and Prevention, *HIV/AIDS Surveillance Report*, 1997, midyear edition, vol. 9, no. 1, p. 16.

14. Centers for Disease Control and Prevention, *HIV/AIDS Surveillance Report*, 1995, year-end edition, p. 5.

15. Ibid.

16. CDC, 1996, p. 17.

17. Ibid., p. 5.

18. Ibid., p. 10.

19. CDC, 1997, p. 15.

20. Daniel Q. Haney, "Dramatic Decline in U.S. AIDS Deaths in 1997," Associated Press, February 3, 1998.

21. "AIDS Study Shows Drop of 26 Percent in Mortality Rate," *Wall Street Journal,* September 12, 1997, p. B8.

22. Author interview with the CDC, April 1998.

23. UNAIDS and WHO, "HIV/AIDS: The Global Epidemic," December 1996, p. 4.

Chapter 3. What Is AIDS?

1. Cimons, Marlene, "Fisher Brings Quiet Voice, Caring Heart to AIDS Controversy," *Los Angeles Times,* February 17, 1994, p. A5.

2. Vargo, Marc E., *The HIV Test* (New York: Pocket Books, 1992), p. 41.

3. "A Physician Guide to HIV Prevention: Sex and HIV Prevention, June 1996," *The Journal of the American Medical Association,* 1997.

4. Anne Novitt-Moreno, "Our Battle Against AIDS; The Fight that Keeps Many Like Magic Johnson Living and Being Positive," *Current Health 2,* vol. 2, February 2, 1996, p. 6.

5. Jon Cohen, "Results on New AIDS Drugs Bring Cautious Optimism," *Science,* February 9, 1996, pp. 755–756.

Chapter 4. Diagnosing HIV Infection

1. Randy Shilts, *And the Band Played On: Politics, People and the AIDS Epidemic* (New York: St. Martin's Press), 1987, 1988, p. 455.

2. Marc E. Vargo, *The HIV Test* (New York: Pocket Books, 1992), p. 41.

3. U.S. Department of Health and Human Services, "New HIV Test Licensed," *FDA Consumer,* vol. 29, March 1995, p. 3.

4. Erich Smith, "New 10-Min. HIV Test Accurate," Associated Press, September 14, 1996.

5. Rebecca Voelker, "Foes of Mandatory Maternal HIV Testing Fear Guidelines Will Lead to Reprisals," *The Journal of the American Medical Association,* vol. 273, April 5, 1995, p. 977.

6. Centers for Disease Control and Prevention, "Recommendations for HIV Testing Services of Inpatients and Outpatients in Acute-Care Hospital Settings," *Morbidity and Mortality Weekly Report, CDC Recommendations and Reports*, vol. 42, no. RR-2, January 15, 1993, p. 4.

Chapter 5. Treatment

1. W. El-Sadr, J. M. Olesks, B. D. Agins et al., *Clinical Practice Guideline No. 7: Evaluation and Management of Early HIV Infection*, AHCPR Publication No. 94-0572 (Rockville, Md.: Agency on Health Care Policy and Research, Public Health Service, U.S. Department of Health and Human Services, January 1994), p. 7.

2. Maggie Fox, "Teens with AIDS Speak to School Children," Reuters NewsMedia Inc., December 2, 1997.

3. Ellen C. Cooper, ed. in chief, *AIDS/HIV Treatment Directory* (New York: American Foundation for AIDS Research, 1996), p. 141.

4. Gary R. Cohan, "Exercise and HIV Infection," *The Advocate*, May 30, 1995, p. 49.

5. Thomas E. Kruger and Thomas R. Jerrells, "Potential Role of Alcohol in Human Immunodeficiency Virus Infection," vol. 6, *Alcohol Health and Research World*, Winter 1992, p. 57.

6. Timothy E. Cote, Robert J. Biggar, and Andrew L. Dannenberg, "Risk of Suicide Among Persons with AIDS: A National Assessment," vol. 268, *The Journal of the American Medical Association*, October 21, 1992, p. 2066.

7. Centers for Disease Control and Prevention. "USPHS/IDSA Guidelines for the Prevention of Opportunistic Infections in Persons Infected with Human Immunodeficiency Virus: A Summary," *Morbidity and Mortality Weekly Report*, July 14, 1995, p. 24.

8. El-Sadr et al., p. 25

9. Jon Cohen, "AIDS Mood Upbeat—For a Change," *Science*, February 17, 1995, p. 959.

10. PR NewsWire, "Pediatric AIDS Foundation Supports New Pediatric HIV/AIDS Treatment Guidelines," September 29, 1997.

11. El-Sadr et al., p. 88.

12. Peter S. Arno and Karyn L. Feiden, *Against the Odds* (New York: HarperCollins Publishers, 1992), pp. 249–251.

13. Nick Siano with Suzanne Lipsett, *No Time to Wait: A Complete Guide to Treating, Managing, and Living with HIV Infection* (New York: Bantam Books, 1993), p. 185.

14. Jon Cohen, "Results on New AIDS Drugs Bring Cautious Optimism," *Science*, February 9, 1996, p. 755.

15. Jon Cohen, "AIDS Therapies: The Daunting Challenge of Keeping HIV Suppressed," *Science*, July 4, 1997, p. 32.

16. Lawrence K. Altman, "AIDS Survival Linked to Doctors' Experience," *The New York Times*, February 1, 1996, p. A11.

17. Valerie E. Stone, George R. Seage III, Thomas Hertz, and Arnold M. Epstein, "The Relation Between Hospital Experience and Mortality for Patients with AIDS," *The Journal of the American Medical Association*, vol. 268, November 19, 1992, p. 2655.

18. Altman, p. A11.

19. C. Wu, "AIDS Progression Depends on the Quality of Care," *Science News*, September 23, 1995, p. 198.

20. Arno and Feiden, p. 57.

21. Lawrence K. Altman, "New AIDS Therapies Arise, But Who Can Afford the Bill?" *The New York Times*, February 6, 1996, p. A1.

22. Ibid., p. B6.

23. Stephanie Stapleton, "New HIV/AIDS Drugs Raise Hopes—But Also Costs," *American Medical News*, August 4, 1997.

24. John G. Bartlett and Ann K. Finkbeiner, *The Guide to Living with HIV Infection* (Baltimore, Md.: The Johns Hopkins University Press, 1993), p. 225.

25. Siano and Lipsett, pp. 125–131.

26 Bartlett and Finkbeiner, p. 210.

27. Ibid., p. 225.

Chapter 6. Prevention

1. Carolyn Thompson, "Experts: HIV Fear Could Wake Up Teens to Their Vulnerability," Associated Press, October 31, 1997.

2. Tresa Baldas, "AIDS Message Is Bitter Pill for Students," *Chicago Tribune*, December 6, 1997.

3. Lilly M. Langer, Rick S. Zimmerman, and Rebecca J. Cabral, "Perceived Versus Actual Condom Skills Among Clients at Sexually Transmitted Disease Clinics," *Public Health Reports*, September–October 1994, p. 683.

4. Neil S. Wenger, Francoise S. Kusseling, and Martin F. Shapiro, "Misunderstandings of 'Safer Sex' by Heterosexually Active Adults," *Public Health Reports*, September–October 1995, p. 618.

5. Kathy A. Fackelmann, "AZT Lowers Maternal HIV Transmission Rate," Science News, vol. 145, February 26, 1994, p. 134.

6. Jeff Stryker, Thomas J. Coates, Pamela DeCarlo, Katherine Haynes-Sanstad, Mike Shriver, and Harvey J. Makadon, "Prevention of HIV Infection: Looking Back, Looking Ahead," *The Journal of the American Medical Association*, vol. 273, April 12, 1995, p. 1143.

7. Lizette Alvarez, "AIDS in Three Portraits: Youths Face the Shadows on Their Horizons," *The New York Times*, March 10, 1996, p. 18.

8. Ralph J. DiClemente and Gina M. Wingood, "A Randomized Controlled Trial of an HIV Sexual Risk-Reduction Intervention for Young African-American Women," *The Journal of the American Medical Association*, October 25, 1995, p. 1271.

9. Adeline M. Nyamathi, Charles Lewis, Barbara Leake, Jacquelyn Flaskerud, and Crystal Bellet, "Barriers to Condom Use and Needle Cleaning Among Impoverished Minority Female Injection Drug Users and Partners of Injection Drug Users," *Public Health Reports*, vol. 110, March–April 1995, p. 166.

10. Deborah L. Shelton, "Not a 'Morning After' Pill," *American Medical News*, August 11, 1997.

11. Alvarez, p. 18.

12. Daniel Romer, "Social Influences on the Sexual Behavior of Youth at Risk for HIV Exposure," *The Journal of the American Medical Association*, vol. 272, August 10, 1994, p. 418C.

13. David R. Holtgrave, Noreen L. Qualls, James W. Curran, Ronald O. Valdiserri, Mary E. Guinan, and William C. Parra, "An Overview of the Effectiveness and Efficiency of HIV Prevention Programs," *Public Health Reports*, vol. 110, March–April 1995, p. 134.

14. Ibid.

15. Nyamathi et al., p. 166.

16. "Coming Clean About Needle Exchange" (editorial), *The Lancet*, vol. 346, November 25, 1995, p. 1377.

17. Facts on File, "New Ads Aimed at Sexually Active Youth," February 3, 1994, p. 66.

18. Kaiser Family Foundation, "The Kaiser Survey on Americans and AIDS/HIV," March 1996, pp. 10–11.

19. U.S. Public Law 102-394, Section 514, *The Lancet*, November 25, 1995.

20. Charles Marwick, "Released Report Says Needle Exchanges Work," *The Journal of the American Medical Association*, vol. 273, April 5, 1995, p. 980.

21. Facts on File, "Needle-Exchange Programs Backed," December 14, 1995, p. 934.

22. Facts on File, "NAS Panel Backs Programs," December 14, 1995, p. 934.

23. Amy Goldstein, "Clinton Supports Needle Exchanges but not Funding," *Washington Post*, April 21, 1998, p. A1.

24. Paul Cotton, "U.S. Sticks Head in Sand on AIDS Prevention," *The Journal of the American Medical Association*, September 14, 1994, p. 756.

25. Holtgrave et al., p. 134.

26. Ibid.

27. Facts on File, "New Ads Aimed at Sexually Active Youth," February 3, 1994, p. 66.

28. "Study Says HIV Spreading Among Young Gay Men," *The Kansas City Star*, Associated Press, February 11, 1996.

29. Holtgrave et al., p. 134.

Chapter 7. Social Implications

1. Susan Goodman, "Darren Sack," *Current Health 2*, November 1993, pp. 8–9.

2. Edward Gilbreath, "Insider Turned Out," *Christianity Today*, February 5, 1996, p. 35.

3. Marc E. Vargo, *The HIV Test* (New York: Pocket Books, 1992), p. 58.

4. UNAIDS and WHO, "Report on the Global HIV/AIDS Epidemic," November 26, 1997.

5. Ibid.

6. "Death by Denial," *The Lancet*, vol. 345, June 17, 1995, p. 1519.

7. Mubarak Dahir, "AIDS Vaccines and Ethical Dilemmas," *Technology Review*, vol. 98, February–March 1995, p. 17.

8. Ibid.

9. UNAIDS and WHO, "HIV/AIDS: The Global Epidemic," November 28, 1996.

10. Paul Cotton, "Human Rights as Critical as Condoms Against HIV," *The Journal of the American Medical Association*, vol. 272, September 14, 1994, p. 758.

11. John S. James, "World Medicine and Western Medicine: The Missing Dialog—Interview, Kaiya Montaocean, Co-Director, Center for Natural and Traditional Medicines," *AIDS Treatment News*, May 17, 1996.

12. Max Essex, "Confronting the AIDS Vaccine Challenge," *Technology Review*, vol. 97, October 1994, p. 22.

13. "Update: HIV-2 Infection Among Blood and Plasma Donors—United States, June 1992–June 1995," *The Journal of the American Medical Association*, vol. 274, October 4, 1995, p. 1007.

14. Cotton, p. 758.

15. Carroll Bogert, "'Making Men Listen,'" *Newsweek*, September 25, 1995, p. 52.

Chapter 8. The Future of AIDS

1. Jon Cohen, "Bumps on the Vaccine Road," *Science*, vol. 265, September 2, 1994, p. 1371.

2. Rebecca Shelton, "AIDS Vaccine: Rhetoric or Reality?" *American Medical News*, August 18, 1997.

3. Wayne C. Koff, "The Next Steps Toward a Global AIDS Vaccine," *Science*, vol. 266, November 25, 1994, p. 1335.

4. Ibid.

5. Shelton.

6. Max Essex, "Confronting the AIDS Vaccine Challenge," *Technology Review*, October 1994, p. 22.

7. Michael L. Nelson, George Chang, Leslie G. Louie, et al., "The Role of Viral Phenotype and CCR5 Gene Defects in HIV-1 Transmission and Disease Progression," *Nature Medicine*, vol. 3, no. 3, March 1997, p. 338.

8. N. J. Deacon, A. Tsykin, A. Solomon, K. Smith, M. Ludford-Menting, D. J. Hooker, D. A. McPhee, A. L. Greenway, A. Ellett, C. Chatfield, V. A. Lawson, S. Crowe, A. Maerz, S. Sonza, J. Learmont, J. S. Sullivan, A. Cunningham, D. Dwyer, D. Dowton, and J. Mills, "Genomic Structure of an Attenuated Quasi Species of HIV-1 from a Blood Transfusion Donor and Recipients," *Science*, vol. 270, November 10, 1995, p. 988.

9. Associated Press, "Gene Mutation Is Second Found to Hinder HIV," August 15, 1997.

10. Sarah Rowland-Jones, "HIV-Specific Cytotoxic T Cells in HIV-Exposed but Uninfected Gambian Women," *The Journal of the American Medical Association*, vol. 273, April 19, 1995, p. 1160F.

11. Janet Raloff, "Baby's AIDS Virus Infection Vanishes," *Science News*, vol. 147, April 1, 1995, p. 196.

12. Jon Cohen, "At Conference, Hope for Success Is Further Attenuated," *Science*, vol. 266, November 18, 1994, p. 1154.

13. Paul Cotton, "International Disunity on HIV Vaccine Efficacy Trials," *The Journal of the American Medical Association*, October 12, 1994, p. 1090.

14. Ibid.

15. Michael Balter, "AIDS Research: Impending AIDS Vaccine Trial Opens Old Wounds," *Science*, vol. 279, no. 5351, January 30, 1998, p. 650.

16. Mubarak Dahir, "AIDS Vaccines and Ethical Dilemmas," *Technology Review*, February–March 1995, p. 17.

17. Ibid.

18. Joseph A. Kovacs et al., "Increases in CD4 T Lymphocytes with Intermittent Courses of Interleukin-2 in Patients with Human Immunodeficiency Virus Infection," *The New England Journal of Medicine*, March 2, 1995, p. 567.

19. Rebecca Voelker, "Cancer Drug May Join the AIDS Arsenal," *The Journal of the American Medical Association*, vol. 274, August 16, 1995, p. 523.

20. Reuters NewsMedia, "Hyperthermia Treatment Safe in Patients with Advanced HIV Infection," March 20, 1996.

21. Rebecca Voelker, "Scientists Zero In on New HIV Microbicides," *The Journal of the American Medical Association*, vol. 273, April 5, 1995, p. 979.

Glossary

AIDS—An abbreviation for acquired immunodeficiency syndrome and generally used in place of the full name. The syndrome is a set of symptoms that develops when a person's immune system becomes unable to fight off disease due to infection by the human immunodeficiency virus (HIV).

AIDS-wasting syndrome—A set of symptoms that are a part of ARC (AIDS-related complex). The symptoms frequently develop in the middle stage of HIV infection, before AIDS sets in. Symptoms include weakness, tiredness, weight loss, diarrhea, and fever.

alternative therapies—Treatments that have not been proved through controlled scientific tests.

anonymous testing—Testing in which the names of the persons being tested are not known or identified.

antibody—A protein molecule that is part of the immune system and that attacks a specific bacterium or virus in the body; a person has numerous antibodies that respond to different microbes.

attenuated—Weakened or decreased. Attenuated viruses may no longer cause disease but may be of use for vaccine development.

AZT—Azidothymidine, the first antiviral drug treatment for HIV; also known as zidovudine (ZDV).

CD4-positive T cells (or helper T cells)—A type of white blood cell that is killed or disabled by HIV infection and that usually signals other parts of the immune system to respond to foreign agents in the body. Counts of CD4-positive T cells provide a powerful indicator of the advance of HIV infection.

clinical trials—Tests of new drugs or vaccines on humans under specific, controlled scientific conditions.

condom—A latex, animal skin, or synthetic sheath that fits snugly over an erect penis, captures ejaculate, and prevents pregnancy. Latex condoms are used to prevent the spread of many sexually transmitted diseases, including HIV, since HIV cannot pass through latex. (HIV can pass through animal skin condoms; synthetic condoms are being tested.)

confidential testing—Testing in which the names of the persons being tested are known. Confidential test results are to be shared only with the person being tested and public health authorities.

contact tracing—A process in which public health authorities seek out persons who have been in contact with a person who has a contagious disease.

contagious—Refers to any disease that can be passed from one person to another.

epidemic—A disease that spreads rapidly through a definable segment of the population, such as in a certain geographic area or in a certain age range.

epidemiologists—People who collect and study information about a disease.

hemophiliac—A person with an inherited blood-clotting disorder. Hemophiliacs often must inject clotting factor derived from blood donations.

heterosexual—A person who is sexually attracted to a person of the opposite sex.

HIV—Abbreviation for human immunodeficiency virus, the retrovirus that causes AIDS. HIV is infectious and contagious, but only through specific kinds of contact.

homosexual—A person who is sexually attracted to a person of the same sex.

immune system—The body's natural defense system against sickness. The system recognizes and neutralizes microbes, then "remembers" them and attacks if the same microbes reappear.

immunity—A natural or acquired resistance to a specific disease. Immunity can be partial or complete, and it can be temporary or long-lasting.

infectious—Referring to a disease that is caused by a microbe.

integrase—An HIV enzyme that helps make viral DNA part of a human cell's DNA. Integrase is one target of drug research.

Kaposi's sarcoma—The most common form of cancer associated with AIDS; previously an uncommon form of cancer that often develops purple or brown lesions on the skin.

lymph—A clear body fluid that carries white blood cells throughout the body.

lymph nodes (or lymph glands)—Small organs located in several places in the body that filter the lymph. Microbes are filtered out for attack by the immune system.

microbe—A microorganism such as a bacterium, virus, protozoan, or fungus.

nucleoside analogs—A class of drugs that slows the progress of HIV infection by interfering with a step in viral reproduction that involves an enzyme called reverse transcriptase.

opportunistic infection—An infection caused by a microbe that usually does not cause disease in a person with a normal immune system.

pandemic—A widespread epidemic.

placebo—An inactive substance administered in place of a drug or other treatment being tested in a clinical trial.

Pneumocystis carinii **pneumonia (PCP)**—A previously rare and life-threatening lung infection caused by protozoa (a group of one-celled animals); a common opportunistic infection among people with AIDS.

protease inhibitors—A class of drugs that slows the progress of HIV infection by interfering with a step in viral reproduction involving an enzyme called protease.

retrovirus—HIV and other viruses that carry their genetic material in the form of RNA and that have the enzyme called reverse transcriptase to convert their RNA into DNA.

reverse transcriptase—An enzyme in HIV and other retroviruses involved in viral reproduction.

tuberculosis (TB)—A bacterial infection spread through airborne droplets when a person with active TB coughs, sneezes, or speaks. TB is particularly hazardous to people with weakened immune systems.

vaccine—A substance that contains components from an infectious agent and that stimulates an immune response. A vaccine thus protects against later infection by the same agent.

viral load—A measure of how much HIV is in a person's blood.

Further Reading

Books

Ford, Michael Thomas. *100 Questions & Answers About AIDS: What You Need to Know Now.* New York: William Morrow & Co., 1993.

Hyde, Margaret O., and Elizabeth H. Forsyth. *AIDS: What Does It Mean to You?* New York: Walker & Co., 1995.

Jussim, Daniel. *AIDS & HIV: Risky Business.* Springfield, N.J.: Enslow Publishers, Inc., 1997.

Kittredge, Mary. *Teens With AIDS Speak Out.* Parsippany, N.J.: Silver Burdett Press, 1992.

Levert, Marianne, *AIDS: A Handbook for the Future.* Brookfield, Conn.: Millbrook Press, Inc., 1996.

Nash, Carol Rust. *AIDS: Choices for Life.* Springfield, N.J.: Enslow Publishers, Inc., 1997.

Newton, David E. *AIDS Issues: A Handbook.* Springfield, N.J.: Enslow Publishers Inc., 1992.

Shilts, Randy. *And the Band Played On.* New York: Penguin Books, 1987, 1988.

Booklets

Centers for Disease Control and Prevention. *HIV/AIDS Surveillance Report,* 1996, year-end edition.

Centers for Disease Control and Prevention. *HIV/AIDS Surveillance Report,* 1997, midyear edition.

Infections Linked to AIDS. National Institute of Allergy and Infectious Diseases, NIH Publication No. 92-2062.

The Kaiser Survey on Americans and AIDS/HIV. Kaiser Family Foundation, March 1996.

Taking the HIV (AIDS) Test. National Institute of Allergy and Infectious Diseases, NIH Publication No. 92-2060.

Testing Positive for HIV. National Institute of Allergy and Infectious Diseases, NIH Publication No. 92-2061.

Articles

Alvarez, Lizette. "AIDS in Three Portraits: Youths Face the Shadows on Their Horizons." *The New York Times*, March 10, 1996.

Chaisson, Richard E., Jeanne C. Keruly, and Richard D. Moore. "Race, Sex, Drug Use, and Progression of Human Immunodeficiency Virus Disease." *The New England Journal of Medicine*, September 24, 1995, p. 751.

Cimons, Marlene. "Fisher Brings Quiet Voice, Caring Heart to AIDS Controversy." *Los Angeles Times*, February 17, 1994, p. A5.

Cohen, Jon. "AIDS Mood Upbeat—For a Change." *Science*, February 17, 1995, p. 958.

————. "Bumps on the Vaccine Road." *Science*, September 2, 1994, p. 1371.

Dahir, Mubarak. "AIDS Vaccines and Ethical Dilemmas." *Technology Review*, February–March 1995, p. 17.

Erben, Rosemarie. "Special AIDS Threat to Women." *World Health*, September 1995, p. 26.

Fackelmann, Kathy A. "AIDS Research: From Vaccines to Safer Sex." *Science News*, August 13, 1994, p. 102.

Goodman, Susan. "Darren Sack." *Current Health 2*, November 1993, pp. 8–9.

Koff, Wayne C. "The Next Steps Toward a Global AIDS Vaccine." *Science*, November 25, 1994, p. 1335.

Marwick, Charles. "Released Report Says Needle Exchanges Work." *The Journal of the American Medical Association*, April 5, 1995, p. 980.

Novitt-Moreno, Anne. "Our Battle Against AIDS; The Fight that Keeps Many Like Magic Johnson Living and Being Positive." *Current Health 2*, February 2, 1996, p. 6.

Raloff, Janet. "Baby's AIDS Virus Infection Vanishes." *Science News*, April 1, 1995, p. 196.

Romer, Daniel. "Social Influences on the Sexual Behavior of Youth at Risk for HIV Exposure." *The Journal of the American Medical Association*, August 10, 1994.

Seligmann, Jean. "The HIV Dating Game." *Newsweek*, October 5, 1992, p. 418C.

Shelton, Deborah L. "Not a 'Morning After' Pill." *American Medical News*, August 11, 1997.

Thompson, Carolyn. "Experts: HIV Fear Could Wake Up Teens to Their Vulnerability." Associated Press, October 31, 1997.

UNAIDS and WHO. "HIV/AIDS: The Global Epidemic." November 28, 1996.

Watters, John K. "HIV Test Results, Partner Notification, and Personal Conduct." *The Lancet*, August 5, 1995, p. 326.

Wenger, Neil S., Francoise S. Kusseling, and Martin F. Shapiro. "Misunderstandings of 'Safer Sex' by Heterosexually Active Adults." *Public Health Reports*, September–October 1995, p. 618.

Index

127